MOUTH FULL OF ASHES

BRIANA MORGAN

PRAISE FOR MOUTH FULL OF ASHES

"*Lost Boys* fans, get ready for your new favorite book. Vivid, heart-wrenching, and bloody, *Mouth Full of Ashes* might breathe eighties nostalgia, but Briana Morgan's vampires offer a fresh as hell take on everyone's favorite creature of the night. A fantastic addition to the vampire genre!"
    - Cat Scully, author of *Jennifer Strange*

"Grief, lust, betrayal and blood. Briana Morgan's *Mouth Full of Ashes* drags its teeth against our flesh, leaving behind hints of nostalgia. These are vampires how I like them, sexy and ruthless."
    - Cynthia Pelayo, Bram Stoker Award Nominee, poet, and author of *Children of Chicago*

"Briana Morgan's *Mouth Full of Ashes* will go for your jugular when you least expect it and will drain you until you have nothing left to give. Razor sharp writing and deeply visceral perfection."
    - Eric Larocca, author of *Things Have Gotten Worse Since We Last Spoke*

"*Mouth Full of Ashes* is *The Lost Boys* for the 2020s. This is a story about loss, love, and lore. Briana's vampires are fast and furious and will leave you lusting for more."
    - Janine Pipe, Splatterpunk Award Nominee, author of *Twisted: Tainted Tales*

ISBN: 9798458163514

Briana Morgan
Atlanta, GA

www.BrianaMorganBooks.com

Trigger warnings: The following work contains scenes of violence
including but not limited to decapitation, stabbing, dislocation, and body
horror. Other sensitive subjects include vomiting, grief, death, violence
against animals, alcohol use, teeth, self-inflicted injuries, car accidents,
drugging, sex, and explicit language. Reader discretion is advised.

To Emma. Thank you.

"A day will come when you think yourself safe and happy, and suddenly your joy will turn to ashes in your mouth, and you'll know the debt is paid."

— *George R.R. Martin*, A Clash of Kings

.

1

If Callie had known what would happen, she would have paid less attention to the radio station, would have focused more on the light in her sister's eyes, on the curve of her mouth as she smiled. On her freckles. On her friendship bracelet, which Callie and her brother had the other pieces of.

But the tragedy of life is never knowing what comes next.

"Would you rather eat only ice cream for the rest of your life, or cake?" Callie's sister Becca asked.

"This is the worst game I've ever played," said Callie's brother Ramsay. "These questions are supposed to be *morbid*, Becs. Come on now."

"Ice cream, for sure," Callie answered. "But Ramsay's right. You're supposed to ask something dark and a little tricky. You know that."

Becca sighed. "It doesn't feel like the right vibe for that. I'm relaxed from a day in the sun."

"You're the only one who didn't get burned," Callie said.

"I reapplied my sunscreen. It's not my fault neither of you listened to me."

"Would you rather die in a car crash or a fire?" Ramsay asked.

"Maybe Becca's right," Callie said. "It's not the right vibe."

Callie and her siblings had stayed at the beach until the sky turned pink and purple as the sun set, and storm clouds loomed on the horizon. All the other beachgoers had left.

Callie and Becca sat back-to-back on the beach blanket. Beside them, Ramsay lounged in a folding chair with his legs stretched out and his feet in the sand. The oldest of the group, Callie had straight, shoulder-length brown hair and intense brown eyes. Her upturned nose scrunched when she laughed. She'd graduated from high school three years earlier and had next to nothing to show for it. She didn't know what to do for a living.

Becca, meanwhile, had dropped out of high school this past year—her and Ramsay's senior year—to pursue cosmetology school. Her face was softer than Callie's, and kinder. They shared the same eyes, but that was where the similarities between them ended. Becca's hair was reddish brown and curled over her collarbone. The wind whipped strands of it around her face.

Ramsay was pure ginger, with unruly red hair, freckles, and brown eyes that looked almost orange in the sunlight. His nose was crooked where a jock had broken it the year before, but rather than tough, it made him look reckless.

They were so white that after a day in the sun, they should've been red as lobsters. Only Ramsay and Callie were sunburned. Becca's sole affliction was her stomach hurt from laughing.

Becca was the first one to address the fast-approaching clouds. "Let's leave before the rain starts."

"Let's stay a little longer," Ramsay replied.

Becca groaned. "That's what you said an hour ago. I have class in the morning, Ram."

He rolled his eyes. "Beauty school barely counts."

Callie laughed, and Becca scoffed, leaning over to punch his arm. "Not enough school for your face," Becca countered.

"You're twins," Callie pointed out.

"Not identical." Becca said, laughing.

Ramsay leaned over and shoved Becca's shoulder. The sun had even burned his scalp, a salmon glow peeking through his hair.

"I'll drive, okay? We'll be back before you turn into a pumpkin, I promise."

Becca rolled her eyes. "I'd feel better if Callie drove."

"Why? Because I drive like a grandma?" Callie asked.

"Doesn't make us love you any less," said Ramsay.

They stood, shook the sand out of the blanket, folded up the chair, grabbed the cooler, and trekked back to Ramsay's Honda Pilot.

Callie offered to drive, but Ramsay declined, sliding into the driver's seat. Becca sat beside her brother in the passenger seat and Callie climbed into the back. Before he could start the engine, Ramsay's phone pinged.

"Storm will be bad. Guess we should've left sooner," he said, frowning down at the screen.

Becca huffed but said nothing as Ramsay started the Pilot. They drove out of the parking lot and onto the main road. Ramsay fiddled with the radio, but Becca pushed his hand away and tuned the station to NPR. The host droned on about unrest in the Middle East, some report that Callie only half listened to.

One minute, the sky was overcast, and Ramsay had no trouble driving. The next, the sky opened, and Ramsay swore as rain flooded the roads. He had a white-knuckled grip on the wheel, but he still smiled at Callie in the rearview mirror. She always scowled at him when he drove. Later, the memory of the faces she'd pulled would rack her with even more guilt.

"You're safe with me," he promised. "Eyes on the road. Hands at ten and two."

"Pay attention," Becca chided.

Ramsay rolled his eyes. On the radio, NPR dissolved into broken static. Becca reached for the dial, but Ramsay swatted her hand away. "Uh-uh, you chose last time. Now it's my—"

"*Ramsay!*"

Callie wasn't sure the scream was hers until Ramsay's eyes widened in the mirror, illuminated by the flash of headlights. They'd traveled over the line into oncoming traffic, close enough to see the terrified people in the other car. Ramsay jerked the wheel to the right and overcompensated. The car screeched, tilted, Becca gasped—

And Callie's world flipped with the car. The front airbags exploded in clouds of white. The screech of metal on pavement, blaring horns, and crash of shattering glass overwhelmed her, and she squeezed her eyes shut.

If only Callie had driven instead.

If only it hadn't rained.

If only they'd left earlier, as they'd planned.

If only one of those factors had been different, Callie wouldn't have blacked out upside-down in the backseat, slammed forward in her seatbelt so hard she cracked a rib.

She woke to the acrid stench of gasoline and motor oil, the sounds of sobbing and sirens, and the copper taste of blood, thick and heavy on her tongue.

Where...?

Callie tried to move, but the seatbelt kept her pinned in place and her ribs protested the effort. Sharp pain flared up her side and spread across her chest. The dashboard pinged —the car thought a door had been left open. Intermittent flashes of red light made the cabin pulse like a heartbeat. Glass tinkled as someone moved. Ramsay groaned, but that was good. He was still alive. Also upside down, he struggled to unclip his seatbelt before giving up.

"Callie," Ramsay croaked.

"Yeah, Ram," she said. "I'm here."

"Becca," he ventured.

Callie froze. Something told her not to look for their sister, that she was better off not knowing, but she had to know. She had to.

"Ram, be careful," she said. "Don't move her too—"

Ramsay touched Becca's shoulder. She leaned out the window, making it impossible to see her head or face. Ramsay shook Becca. No response.

He looked back at Callie, eyes pleading, asking what neither one of them wanted to answer.

"Try again." Callie's voice was hoarse. "A little harder."

"Becca." Ramsay shook her shoulder more insistently. Becca made no sound, and he tried again. "Becs, please, I need you. *We* need you."

Callie's vision tunneled. She fought the urge to pass out. She had to know what had happened to Becca, if she was—

Alive.

Ramsay surged forward in his seat. He grabbed Becca's

shoulder with both hands and pulled her into the cabin. She slumped against the dashboard.

Becca's head was gone.

Callie clasped her hands over her mouth to stifle a scream and looked out the window. The red light continued to flash, draping her sister's severed head in a crimson glow as it lay in a sea of broken safety glass, revealing an expression of terror on Becca's face that equaled Callie's own.

2

I n the three months since the accident, Callie's mom Susan had upended the family's lives and moved them out of the city. Callie was twenty-one, and Ramsay was eighteen. They could've stayed behind. But they were as low on funds as they were on morale, and their mother needed them. So they went.

Here in Neap Bay, California, where Susan had grown up, the air smelled like fried food, cigarettes, and booze. Callie and Ramsay stood in line to get tickets to enter the Starlight Boardwalk, where their mother worked. It was the only decent place to hang out in Neap Bay unless they wanted to spend money at the strip mall.

Callie wore cutoff denim shorts, a white T-shirt, and red Converse sneakers. Ramsay's ensemble consisted of tan shorts, a plaid button-down with the sleeves rolled up, and Birkenstocks.

"We should've asked Mom if she could get us in," said Callie. The salty breeze coming off the ocean mussed her newly bleached blonde bob and settled on her skin. Neap Bay was drying her out. "That would've been easier."

"And cheaper," said Ramsay. "But Mom can't know we're here."

Callie frowned. "Why not?"

"Because then she'd ask me why I wanted to meet up with some stranger from the Internet," he hissed.

"Wait," Callie said. "You're giving him a second chance? Ramsay, you *told* me—"

"I know what I told you," he said. "How else was I supposed to get you to drive me here?"

Callie sighed. "So... there *isn't* a showing of *The Lost Boys* on a big screen over the boardwalk."

"Nope, but if I'm lucky, you might get to see some biting."

She wished she had something she could've hit him with. "I can't believe you."

"Really?" he asked.

"Okay, I can. I just don't want to."

Callie was an avid horror fan whose latest fascination was vampires. The last movie they watched before Becca died had been *The Hunger*, which had sparked Callie's thirst for more vampire content. In the months since, she'd devoured everything from *Fright Night* to *The Lost Boys* with no plans of slowing down.

"Couldn't have gotten here without you," said Ramsay. "I'm doing the whole 'no driving' thing now, remember?"

"The guy who stood you up last time doesn't have a car?" asked Callie. "Yet another point against him."

"He's *nice*," Ramsay said, "and he's not bad to look at. Met him on Grindr. Give him a shot."

"I guess if you are, I have no choice," she said.

As the line moved up, Callie's eyes fell on the telephone pole beside her. It was littered with chewed-up gum and posters of young people that cried MISSING at the top.

She'd seen some like them the few times she went into town, but the amount of them surprised her. Neap Bay had its share of secrets.

"Earth to Callie," Ramsay said. She snapped out of her reverie, realizing her inattention had created a gap in the line. Ramsay had moved up without her. She offered him a sheepish look and scooted up beside him.

They'd finally reached the ticket booth. The attendant took their money and slid their tickets out from under the window. Callie pocketed the change and examined the ticket carefully: STARLIGHT BOARDWALK. ADMIT ONE. NO REENTRY PERMITTED.

Ramsay led her through the crowd and past the turnstiles, which clicked loudly as Callie pushed through them. At the front of the boardwalk, two gilded posts marked the entrance. An enormous blue banner stretched between them, with gold letters that screamed STARLIGHT BOARDWALK: A GALAXY OF DELIGHTS AWAITS YOU, and stars embroidered all around. Callie doubted the boardwalk held a planet's worth of attractions, let alone a galaxy.

"Where are you meeting him?" she asked. The buzz and chatter of people, rides, and games made it difficult for Callie to hear herself think.

Even Ramsay, who wasn't a quiet talker, had to raise his voice. "Where am I meeting who?"

"This mystery man."

"His *name* is Jabari. And he asked if I could meet him right outside the haunted house." Ramsay barely dodged two women pushing a stroller. They shot him a glare. He ignored it. "He works here, actually. Part of the boardwalk."

Callie raised an eyebrow. "He's a game attendant?"

"Kind of."

"Jesus," Callie said. "Ramsay... tell me he isn't a drug dealer or something. What if he's unstable?"

"Paranoid much?" Ramsay asked. "It's nothing like that. He does some sleight of hand. No biggie."

"A magician? That's worse."

Ramsay didn't answer her. Instead, he pulled his cell phone out and scrolled through his text messages. Nearby, a car backfired. Callie and Ramsay both flinched, then locked eyes.

"I'm coming with you," she said. "Let me scope him out, and if he's chill, I'll leave."

"I don't need a babysitter," Ramsay grumbled.

"And *I* didn't need to be your taxi," she said.

For a moment, they stared at each other. Sometimes, when Callie looked at him, all she could see was Becca. She brushed the pang of grief away.

"I'm not coming back here a third time," she said.

"I know you aren't," he answered. "Let's go find Jabari."

"It's just weird," said Callie. "Yesterday, he stands you up. Today, he acts like nothing's wrong. He whistles, you come running. What if he's a catfish?"

"I'll never know if we don't meet him. Come *on*, Callie."

Callie shoved her hands in the pockets of her jeans and stared down at her red Converse shoes as they headed toward the haunted house attraction. She hated pouting, but damn it, Ramsay was being ridiculous. He'd made her an accessory to his bullshit crusade. She wanted to get back in the car and leave his ass at the boardwalk so she could go home and sleep. To his credit, Ramsay said nothing as they walked. Maybe he knew better than to press his luck.

A long, low whistle caught Callie's attention as they neared the attraction. She stopped alongside Ramsay, lifting her gaze to meet the whistler's. He was a tall Black man with hooded brown eyes, close-cropped hair, and a row of golden earrings all along his left ear. He arched an eyebrow and grinned at Ramsay like the Cheshire cat.

Something in his smile chilled Callie's blood.

"Hey, stranger," the man purred.

Ramsay smiled. His fingers twitched at his sides. "Hey yourself."

The man came closer to them. He was still beaming at Jabari, but the smile left his eyes when he looked at Callie.

"Your sister?" he asked.

"You must be the jerk who stood my brother up," she said.

Jabari gave a short, sharp laugh of surprise. "Seems she's got teeth. Ram, you never said that."

Ram. Callie, Becca, and their mom were the only ones who'd ever called him that. Hearing the nickname in some rude man's mouth was a slap in the face. Her eyes narrowed, and she tugged on Ramsay's sleeve again, not letting go this time.

"She doesn't get out much," Ramsay said. Jabari leaned in and pressed a kiss to Ramsay's cheek—and then her brother blushed.

Imagine if Becca could see him like this, Callie thought. *Happy, after so much pain.* An ache bloomed in her chest.

"I'm Callie," she tried again.

"Jabari. Good to meet you." He took Ramsay's hand. "Let's go inside."

A teenage girl stood behind a podium at the attraction's entrance. The enormous double doors beside her swung open, and she gestured toward them. "Head on in."

Jabari and Ramsay went in first. Callie followed.

The haunted house smelled like urine, sweat, and mildew. Acrid fog from machines curled around Callie's ankles as she trailed behind Jabari and Ramsay. They still held hands. Overhead blacklight bars cast an otherworldly glow over the trio and their clothes, brightening Callie's T-shirt so that it was almost blinding. Canned clown laughter blared through unseen speakers. Callie tried not to trip over a cord on the floor half hidden by black electrical tape.

"Seems like a safety issue to have power cords strewn everywhere," she muttered.

"What?" Ramsay asked without turning his head.

Callie was surprised he'd heard her. "It smells like piss in here."

"Wouldn't rule it out," Jabari replied.

A hydraulic hiss preceded a zombie popping up in front of them, uttering a guttural moan. Ramsay jumped and cried out, latching onto Jabari. Horror movies put Ramsay to sleep, so his behavior was suspicious.

Callie didn't have long to ponder the strangeness. The toe of her Converse caught on a wire, and she went down, scraping up her hands and knees. Sharp heat spread from the injuries, and she swore.

"Callie?" Ramsay tugged Jabari to a stop. He turned, and even in the dim light, Callie saw his brow furrow. "You okay?" Ramsay asked.

"Yeah, I think so." She pulled herself to a seated position, assessing the damage. Nothing was broken. Blood trickled from her left knee, and it smarted like hell, but it would heal. Her hands would bruise, maybe. It wasn't too bad.

Jabari advanced toward her, sneering, violence flashing in his eyes—before he shook himself and stopped just short of Callie.

After looking from Ramsay to Callie again, Jabari's face softened. "You're bleeding."

Callie checked her knee again. "It's not too bad. Should stop in a minute."

Ramsay brushed past Jabari to kneel beside Callie. If anyone else came into the haunted house, they couldn't linger like this.

"You want to go?" he asked.

"I thought that's what we were doing," she replied. He stretched out a hand, and she let him help her to her feet. "Aren't we heading toward the exit?"

"More or less," Jabari said, even though Callie wasn't speaking to him.

"There should be an emergency exit up ahead," he added.

Ramsay took out his phone and turned on the flashlight. The pop-up zombie mechanism gave another hydraulic hiss, barely giving anyone time to brace themselves before the zombie reappeared with a prerecorded groan. Ramsay and Callie both jumped, but Jabari didn't.

Somehow, he'd gotten closer to Callie. He was taller than she'd realized. A little more imposing.

Ramsay steadied her with a hand on her waist. Gratitude bloomed through Callie's chest.

"Which way?" Ramsay asked Jabari.

Jabari looked at the zombie, eyebrows scrunching together. He jerked his head to the right. "This way."

Ramsay kept his flashlight beam trained on the ground ahead of them as they walked so that there wouldn't be any more cord-tripping incidents. Jabari pushed on what had looked like a wall to Callie, and it became a curtain that gave way under his touch.

Callie and Ramsay followed Jabari through the curtain and down a corrugated-metal hallway toward a bright-red EXIT sign. Jabari pushed the handle on the door, and it swung outward. The smell of fried food and the sounds of cicadas and people shouting poured into the building. Jabari held the door open for Ramsay and Callie, and the red-haired attendant outside shot them a confused look as they exited.

"That's for emergencies," she said.

"I'm bleeding," Callie said. "Besides that, nobody's in there."

"You're bleeding? Oh, shit." The girl crept closer to Callie. She looked about Callie's age only several inches shorter. "Did something happen in there?"

"She tripped over a power cord," Jabari said, trying to smooth things over. "Do you have a kit out here?"

"A kit?" The girl paled. "I... I'm supposed to, but I don't think—"

"Never mind." Jabari looked to Callie. "You can come with me. I have one in my trailer. We'll get you patched up." He looked at Ramsay. "You can wait here."

Ramsay frowned. "I want to help."

"I think I can handle it, Ram." Once again, Jabari's tone was warm, but it had an edge to it that turned Callie's stomach. The more time she spent around Jabari, the less she liked him. "The trailer's pretty small, and I don't want anyone getting claustrophobic."

"It's not a problem," Callie said. "Besides, I want him with me."

Something shifted in Jabari's face. His eyes darkened. When he spoke again, his voice was rough. "You don't think I'll take good care of her?"

Ramsay blinked. "Th-that's not what—"

"Because I'm boardwalk trash? Is that it?" Jabari's nostrils flared. "You think I'm an idiot because I dropped out of school?"

"He didn't say that," Callie countered.

"He didn't have to."

"Jabari," Ramsay started. "Forget it. Callie and I—"

"Get the fuck out of here with that attitude." Jabari scowled. "Thinking you're better than everyone else."

Ramsay frowned. Callie wanted to change the subject, but she didn't know what to say. Maybe Jabari had a point. Maybe they should leave.

"Come on, Ram. Let's go find Mom."

His mouth opened like he wanted to say something, but his shoulders slumped, and he only nodded. Without looking at Jabari, Ramsay shoved his hands in his pockets and pivoted. As he walked off, Callie followed. She half expected Jabari to relent, apologize, and stop them, but he didn't. She didn't think her mom could make Ramsay feel better, but it was worth a shot.

Besides, if she didn't distract herself, Callie swore she'd run back and knock Jabari upside the head.

3

Callie heard their mom before she saw her, calling out food orders to a table of patrons. Upon arriving in Neap Bay, she'd secured a position as a part-time waitress at the coming Starlight Boardwalk. Callie's mom had been a waitress for as far back as Callie remembered. Callie and Ramsay didn't know how their mom could just go about her business like she hadn't survived the worst loss of her life. Unlike Callie and Ramsay, their mother seldom cried—not in front of anyone, at least —or said a word about Becca.

Some part of her was still in denial. Callie couldn't say she blamed her.

At the sight of her children, Susan's face lit up. Callie had never pictured her mom as a boardwalk worker, but here she was, doing the damn thing. Since their father walked out on them when Callie was eight, their mother had taken any job she could get to keep the family afloat. It couldn't have been easy raising three children alone, but Susan had done it. Some days, Callie thought her mom deserved a medal.

Susan looked Callie over, noticed her injuries, and paled. "Oh, Cal, you're bleeding. Hang on a sec." She looked around for help. "Derek, could you come out here? Derek! It's an emergency."

An attractive white man in his forties, around Susan's age, stumbled out from behind a curtain. He wore glasses that failed to obscure striking brown eyes. Callie wondered why they were so striking. They were just brown. Nothing to report.

"Susan," Derek started. "What's—what happened here?"

"Derek," Susan said breathlessly. "These are my kids, Calliope and Ramsay. Callie's hurt herself."

"Mom, I'm fine," said Callie.

Susan ignored her. "You're not in pain or anything? I'm guessing you fell somewhere." She looked at Ramsay. "What about you, love? Are you all right?"

"Callie busted her ass in the haunted house," he said. "But me? Yeah, I'm all right."

Derek still hadn't answered Susan. He stared at her, but not in a creepy way. In fact, if Callie wasn't seeing things, she could've sworn Derek had a crush on her mom. He wouldn't have been the first. Susan had wavy red hair that curled around her shoulders and brown eyes, like Callie's. Unlike Callie, though, her eyes were framed by long lashes that hadn't gotten sparser with age. A few streaks of gray popped out at her temples.

Susan offered Derek a smile. "Could you cover for me while I grab the first-aid kit?"

Derek nodded, like he wanted to do that and more for her. Callie felt a little sick. The guy could at least pretend to be cool.

Susan went back behind the curtain Derek had appeared from. He went over to her table without another glance at the teenagers and started talking to Susan's customers. While they chatted, Ramsay pulled Callie into a side conversation, keeping his voice low in an uncharacteristic display of self-control and subtlety.

"Guy has the hots for Mom, don't you think?"

"Oh, without a doubt." Callie flexed her leg and winced. She would have some bruises.

"How long has it been since she dated what's his face?" Ramsay asked.

"Mark?" Callie asked. "Or Bruno?"

"Shit," Ramsay said. "I forgot about Bruno."

Callie arched an eyebrow. "Handlebar mustache, thick Southern accent?"

"The redneck? Damn. How could I forget him?"

"I dunno. Don't think he'd forget you."

"It's hard to forget the only gay kid you think you've ever met," Ramsay said.

"Me and my passing privilege thank you for your bigot-slaying service."

"Well, he needed someone to tell him off. Mom wouldn't do it." He reached up and rubbed the back of his neck. "It's not right that she keeps going off with all these bad dudes. Her shit detector's broken."

"You're one to talk," Callie said.

He scowled. "What's that supposed to mean?"

Callie sighed. "Your new guy—Jabari—is weird, okay? I mean, I still can't get over the way he looked at me after I started bleeding. I can't stop thinking about how weird he was about trying to get me alone." She paused. So far, he hadn't stopped her. That was progress. "I don't think Becca would have liked him."

"Calliope," Ramsay said. "Shut the fuck up."

Callie winced. "Sorry."

"Mark was a year ago. Bruno... like two." She offered him a smile, but he didn't look at her. "How old do you think Derek is? Could he have a deep, dark secret?"

"What, like he's a serial killer?"

"Or maybe a werewolf. Something."

Susan returned with the first-aid kit. She cleaned Callie's wounds with some antiseptic solution that stung when it met oxygen. Callie swore and Susan didn't even reprimand her. As she put the last band-aid on Callie, she sighed.

"I'm working almost all night tonight. Can you two keep out of trouble until morning at least?"

"No promises," said Ramsay.

"I should've known you'd say that. I'd appreciate the effort, though, if you could manage."

"I'll watch him, Mom." Callie reached out and ruffled Ramsay's hair. He groaned. She pretended she hadn't heard it and smiled at him. "We'll behave, won't we?"

"I'm new in town," he said. "How much trouble could I get into?"

"Let's not find out." Susan got to her feet, brushed her uniform off, and appraised the siblings. She tilted her head and clicked her tongue. "If I didn't know any better, I'd say you two looked like angels."

"Hopefully no one knows any better," Ramsay said.

"Who could tell but me?" Susan asked. She glanced at Derek, who was still staring at her. "It's... been a weird night. Already. There's a full moon out, which means things only stand to get weirder. If you're going home, stay in. It will make me feel better. Would you do that for me?"

"That guy totally wants to bang you," Ramsay said.

Callie rolled her eyes. Susan cracked a smile, but it wasn't convincing. "I'll take that as a yes. There's money in

the kitchen if you want to order a pizza, okay? Text me when
you get home."

"You just want us to leave you alone with Derek,"
Ramsay said.

"She gets it," Callie said. "And Mom's right. We should
head out. I need to clean these scrapes and shit."

"Watch your language," Susan said.

"Okay, yeah, we're going." Callie let her mom hug her,
then Ramsay, before they stood and prepared to head out.
Derek was still watching them, and he was doing a poor job
of pretending he wasn't. Since their mother still had said
nothing bad about Derek, maybe she liked the attention.
Hell, maybe it was good for her. She hadn't been with
anyone in a long time. God knew flirting—and dating—
could provide a distraction from the hellscape that had been
their life this year.

Callie was about to tell her mom to have a good rest of
her shift when she felt the heat of someone else's gaze. She
touched Ramsay's arm to warn him—but he was already
staring at the source of the problem.

Not far away, at the edge of the food area, Jabari hung
back in the shadows. As Callie and Ramsay looked back at
him, he didn't wave. He didn't smile. He didn't look away.

A chill crawled down Callie's spine. Still, she did her
best to keep her unease off her face. She grabbed Ramsay's
arm. Thankfully, he didn't react. "We'll head out now, Mom.
Love you."

"Love you," Ramsay echoed. For the time being, he
seemed content to let Callie lead him.

"Love you both," said Susan. "So, so much."

"Okay, ew," said Ramsay. He tried to come across as
joking, but his tone fell flat. Callie wondered if he was as
creeped out and unnerved by Jabari now as she was.

Callie steered Ramsay away from their mother, away from Derek, and away from Jabari and his creepy prying eyes. They made to the front of the boardwalk, through the turnstiles, and into the parking lot with no interruption. The only sounds outside were the hum of engines starting and the droning of cicadas.

Ramsay stood beside the passenger door, waiting for Callie to unlock the car. He didn't make eye contact.

She took her keys out of her purse, turning them over in her hands. "I don't think you should spend any more time with him."

"Can we not do this now? Unlock the car."

Callie sighed. She unlocked the car, got in, and waited for Ramsay. They both closed their doors, and she started the engine. Once they had their seatbelts on, she hesitated. "He's not a good guy, Ram. I know he's nice to look at and maybe he makes you feel good sometimes, but you deserve better."

"He's a dick," Ramsay agreed. "Don't know what got into him. He seemed chill in his messages and in person at first, and then you fell in the haunted house, and everything changed."

"Not sure what the hell that was."

Callie backed out of the parking space and drove out of the lot. Her hands and knee still stung, but not enough to concern her. They were just scrapes. She had bled on her clothes somewhere, but if she couldn't get the stains out, it wasn't a big deal.

Blood. That was why Jabari had freaked out.

"Maybe he's not good with blood," she remarked.

"What?" Ramsay asked.

"Jabari. He was okay until I fell. Until he saw the blood. Maybe it triggered him somehow."

"He didn't faint or anything, Cal. He wasn't squeamish. I don't think that's it."

"The timing makes sense."

"Yeah, but that's it. I don't know, maybe he couldn't keep up the nice guy facade any longer." He stared out the window as they headed down the road. "Ugh. I'm such a moron."

"You are not a moron. He's good at what he does. Whatever that means."

Ramsay leaned his seat back, closed his eyes, and said nothing along the way. He'd fallen asleep. She couldn't stop thinking about how much he looked like Becca in the moonlight, and the more she thought about it, the sharper the pain grew. Callie wanted to blast some metal and scream, but Ramsay needed rest. She didn't have the heart to wake him yet.

It wasn't a long drive to their house from the boardwalk though, and she parked the car and turned it off only fifteen minutes later. The engine ticked as it cooled.

Callie shook Ramsay's shoulder. "Hey, dude. We're here."

"I was thinking about her," he mumbled.

"Who?"

"Becca." His eyes fluttered open, and he offered her a sleepy half-smile. "She would have kicked Jabari's ass for talking to me like that."

"No, she wouldn't. She would've been obsessed with him, too."

Ramsay wrinkled his nose at her. "I'm not obsessed."

"Whatever you say, man. Let's go inside."

They made the trek up the front steps and onto the porch. Moths circled the light outside the door. Callie and Ramsay were careful not to let the bugs inside with them.

Without turning on the lights, Callie headed to her

bedroom, grabbed a pillow and blanket off the bed, and brought them to Ramsay on the couch. Since they'd moved in, he'd been sleeping in the living room. Some of Becca's old things sat unattended in his room, and if Callie had to guess, he couldn't sleep near them. In the living room, he'd switched on the lamp and sat against the cushions with his eyes closed. When she dropped the pillow and blanket onto his lap, he jumped.

"Jesus," Ramsay said.

"Sorry," she replied. "Didn't think you'd be asleep."

"I wasn't asleep. I was thinking."

"Either way." She smiled. "It's been a long night. I'm gonna head to bed. You'll be okay out here?"

"Yeah. If I get scared, I'll crawl into bed with you."

Callie rolled her eyes, and he grinned at her. It was the first time she'd seen him happy since leaving Jabari behind, and she was thrilled she'd made it happen. Maybe the night wasn't a complete loss.

"Hey," she said.

"Hey what?"

"I love you. A lot."

"I love you too, you goober. Go to bed."

Ramsay swung the pillow at her, and she dodged, laughing. "If I weren't so tired, I'd beat your ass in a pillow fight right now."

"Tomorrow is another day," he said. "Goodnight, Cal."

"Night, Ram. Let me know if you need anything."

He set the pillow down and stretched out on the couch. With her back turned, she heard him switch the television on and turn the volume down. He couldn't sleep without noise, and cartoons chased the nightmares away.

Callie went back to her bedroom and closed the door. She pulled the chain on her bedside lamp, illuminating the framed photograph on her nightstand. In it, she stood on the beach between Becca and Ramsay with her arms around both. All of them sported wide, easy smiles. Becca wore a high-waisted yellow bikini with black-striped bottoms that Ramsay had said made her look like a bee. Becca had liked bees.

Callie's heart twisted. She pulled the chain to turn the light off, put her face in her hands, and cried.

4

Thunder ripped Callie out of a nightmare. She sat bolt upright, clutching the sheets to her chest, face slick with sweat. It trickled down her cheeks, mingling with her tears. Though the nightmare was familiar, it was no less frightening. But it wasn't a nightmare. It was a memory.

Almost every night since it had happened, she relived the accident. Snatches of conversation in the aftermath swirled inside her head.

"Dead on impact."

"Likely didn't feel a thing."

"So young, it's such a shame…"

"Closed casket."

"Poor Ramsay. They say it's worse for twins."

That didn't mean it hurt any less for Callie. The other one. The forgotten sister.

Callie stifled a sob with a hand against her mouth. She didn't want to wake Ramsay again. It wasn't the first time she'd had the nightmare, and it wouldn't be the last. Ramsay had nightmares too.

Callie's fingers went to the bracelet on her left wrist. There was only bare skin. Callie's pulse quickened and her stomach dropped into her ass. Where the hell was Becca's bracelet?

She threw off the covers and swung her legs over the side of the bed. The lamp's chain was cold in her hand as she pulled it and filled the room with light. Maybe the bracelet had fallen off while she was sleeping. Sweating, she swept her hand across the blankets and under the fitted sheet. Nothing. Callie even shook the pillow out of its case and let it fall to the floor beside the bed.

All that lay on her nightstand was an orange bottle filled with ADHD meds, her cell phone plugged into its charger, and a dog-eared copy of *Twilight* she doubted she'd ever get through. It had been Becca's favorite book once, and in the wake of losing the bracelet, Callie felt a twinge of guilt-ridden panic as she looked at it.

Even when she showered, she kept the bracelet on. The interwoven threads and dangling silver charm, a piece of a heart that said FRIENDS, was one of the few things she had left of Becca. If she'd lost the bracelet...

No. Callie refused to consider it. She couldn't have lost the bracelet. It was somewhere in the house, or maybe it had fallen off in the car.

Callie cracked open her bedroom door and padded out into the hallway. The house was steeped in darkness save a sliver of light coming in through the living room blinds. No matter how hard she tried, Callie could never get them fully closed. The light stretched over the couch and spread over Ramsay's face. He snored softly. No point in waking him up. The bracelet could still be close by. She didn't want to worry him.

For a minute, she stood there watching him sleep. She

felt like a creep, but it calmed her. Rain pelted the windows. Lightning flashed outside, followed by another crack of thunder. Callie put a hand against the wall to steady herself. How many rainy nights had she, Becca, and Ramsay fallen asleep on the couch together in the middle of a movie marathon?

Callie's heart ached, and once again, she touched her bare wrist. Her gaze swept over the coffee table, across the floor, and back to the couch. No sign of the bracelet anywhere. Perhaps Ramsay lay on top of it, or it had fallen between the couch cushions, but she could've sworn she remembered twisting the ends of it at the boardwalk—

Damn. That was it. She must have lost it at the boardwalk.

"Jesus Christ," she muttered. So much for a good night's sleep.

With a sigh, Callie crept back to her bedroom, changed clothes, and grabbed her cell phone from the nightstand. It felt wrong to leave Ramsay behind, but she didn't want to wake him.

She was also glad their mother wasn't home yet. Her superpower was hearing floorboards creak whenever her children tried to sneak out. It was almost always the twins who got caught. Callie looked again at the picture on her nightstand and felt a pang of regret.

If Ramsay found out she'd lost Becca's bracelet, he'd flip. He still had his, but Becca losing hers meant losing a tie to Becca.

The cranberry-rust stain at the edge of the white area rug in front of her bed caught her eye. Becca had spilled a glass of wine there. If Callie really scrubbed, she could get the stain out, but did she want to?

Before she lost her nerve or had a breakdown, Callie

grabbed her keys, turned off the bedside lamp, and headed out of the house.

CALLIE HAD NOW PULLED into the Starlight Boardwalk's parking lot two more times than she'd wanted to. The rain had stopped, but Callie dodged puddles as she got out of her car. The humidity choked her. Few cars filled the spaces beside hers, although the lights beyond the lot were just as bright as they'd been earlier. Another girl got out of her car. They locked eyes before the other girl turned and headed into the boardwalk.

A muffled voice boomed an announcement over the intercom as Callie made her way toward ticketing. If she kept coming back here without her mom's help, she was going to go broke.

"Closes in an hour," the ticket worker said.

"I know," said Callie.

"All right. It's your money."

The worker slid her ticket over. Callie took the ticket and pushed through the turnstiles. With most people gone, the hum of machinery for the rides and attractions filled the empty air. A few couples milled around, but at midnight, the boardwalk was nearly deserted. The canvas roof over the carousel creaked and rustled in the wind. Most of the food stalls were shuttered. Everything smelled like hot oil, stale beer, and sugar. Callie's stomach turned, but she pressed on, heading toward the haunted house. The bracelet had been on her wrist when she fell—she remembered worrying that she'd gotten blood on it.

A sharp laugh behind her made her jump. Callie

whirled around and saw someone she recognized along with some people she didn't.

"Long time no see," Jabari said. He stood in a loose semi-circle with two feminine-presenting people and one masculine-presenting one. The first woman was tall, slender, and white, with bleach-blonde hair like Callie's, but shaved on one side. She wore a black bralette, a floral skirt, combat boots, and fishnets. The other woman was Black, with long braids threaded with gold ribbons. Metallic beads clicked through some strands as she tilted her head to look at Callie. She wore a flowy black dress and a wide-brimmed black hat that made her look witchy. Both women had septum rings. Both stared at her.

As for the man, he was shorter than Jabari. He had messy, dark hair and sleepy blue eyes, but he emanated power, confidence, magnetism. He wore dark jeans, boots, and a leather jacket open over a mesh shirt. Someone had tattooed HEDONIST in red letters over his heart.

The man's eyes sparkled as he studied her. He had both arms thrown over the women's shoulders. Callie was self-conscious.

"Who's this?" the man asked Jabari. The sounds of the boardwalk faded until Callie couldn't focus on anything but him.

"Ramsay's sister," said Jabari. "Callie, think it was."

Callie bristled. It was rude to talk about her like she wasn't there, and ruder for him to act like he couldn't remember her name, especially when he'd been so creepy toward her earlier.

"I'm sure she can speak for herself," the man said.

"Yeah," she said. "I'm Callie."

"Nice to meet you, Callie. I'm Elijah." He clasped her hand it and raised it to his lips before dropping a kiss on her knuckles. Despite herself, Callie blushed. Elijah winked before he let go of her hand.

"Name's Maeve," said the first woman, the one with the bleach-blonde hair.

"Tahlia," said the second, the one with the golden threads.

"I... I lost a bracelet here." Callie touched her bare wrist. "It's handmade and irreplaceable."

"This is the last place you remember having it?" Elijah asked. "What does it look like, darling?"

Darling. His use of a pet name took Callie aback, but not for long "It's made of thread, red and yellow. It's dingy from me wearing it all the time. And there's a silver charm on it that says FRIENDS."

"BEST FRIENDS?" Maeve butted in.

"BEST FRIENDS FOREVER," Callie said. "It's a heart split into three." It felt like admitting an embarrassing secret.

"Maybe you dropped it in the haunted house," Jabari said. He looked like he wanted to say something else, but Elijah cut his eyes at him.

Callie chewed the inside of her cheek. That was the most likely answer, but she doubted she'd find it there now. Perhaps someone had picked it up, or they had cleaned the haunted house out, or even—

"Lost and found." Callie's gaze fell on Elijah. "There's a lost and found, right? Can you take me there?"

Elijah frowned. "I'm afraid there isn't. Boardwalk rules follow a finders-keepers philosophy."

Callie's frown mirrored his. She shifted her attention to Jabari. "You don't remember seeing it, do you? After I fell? When we left the house?"

Jabari opened his mouth, then closed it. What was he going to say? Why didn't he just say it?

Elijah's tongue darted out to wet his lips. Callie let her eyes linger on his mouth for longer than she should have. The man had nice lips. Full. Inviting.

"Why don't you come hang out with us?" Elijah asked. "We can help look for the bracelet. In the meantime, perhaps we can convince you to have some fun, hm?"

Callie understood it wasn't a great idea to go anywhere with this group of near strangers who outnumbered her and knew the boardwalk better than she did. But when Elijah spoke, his golden tone made her believe him. It made Callie want to give him anything he wanted. Besides, he had a point. Maybe she should loosen up.

Callie's thoughts raced, along with her heart. The edges of her vision blurred. Her head felt heavy. Foggy.

Why had she come to the boardwalk? She had been looking for... something she'd lost.

Elijah smiled at her again, and it didn't matter anymore.

He anchored her to the present and promised her the future.

"I'll go with you," she said.

For a moment, something dark flitted across Elijah's features. Something predatory. But he replaced it with another charming smile and a twinkle in his eyes.

5

Callie had almost expected them to take her to a tent, so when they led her past the parking lot to a group of camper vans at the edge of the woods, she was pleasantly surprised.

The embers of a campfire glowed in the center of the group of vans. Metal folding chairs with mesh backs surrounded the fire and a red-sided cooler sat against a chair. A few cigarette butts littered the ground and Callie skirted around them as Elijah and the others led her toward the seating.

Elijah motioned at Jabari, who went to the fire without further prompting. Jabari knelt, took out a lighter, and poked the embers with a stick. Tahlia and Maeve lowered themselves into adjacent chairs. Elijah remained standing with Callie. He seemed taller somehow, shoulders thrown back, chin raised, eyes blazing. Callie felt a twinge of nervousness as he looked her over again.

"It's quiet back here," she said. The campground was far enough from the boardwalk that it was tucked into the forest and the chirping cicadas drowned out the sounds of people and machinery. They were far from the boardwalk's floodlights, and the only illumination came from the moon and amber string lights on the campers.

The moonlight glanced off the sharp planes of Elijah's face and cast shadows under his cheeks, across his mouth.

"How are your injuries?" he asked.

Callie's brow furrowed. His gaze drifted down her legs, hesitated at her knees, then jumped back up to her face. Realization dawned on her. "Oh, the scrapes from where I fell. I guess Jabari told you."

"Word travels fast. Not much else to do but talk."

"I'm fine. I mean, it's nothing major. Bled a little, but not too badly."

"Blood doesn't bother you?" The corners of Maeve's mouth twitched.

"Not really." Callie looked from Maeve to Jabari, who had lit the fire and kept it going. Their eyes... something in their eyes made it difficult to focus, and she had to keep her wits about her. "Can't say I've ever been squeamish."

"Good to know." Elijah's voice was low and smooth.

"So," Callie asked, "where do you work? What do you do at the boardwalk?"

She felt, rather than saw, Elijah's smile falter. "We're jacks of all trades. Renaissance people." He shifted his weight from one foot to the other, and the movement caught Callie's attention. His boots were heeled, and high—she hadn't noticed earlier.

"Pickpockets," said Jabari. So, that was what Ramsay had meant by *sleight of hand.*

Elijah laughed. "Guilty. Callie, please. Sit."

She moved to the empty chair and sat. His voice compelled her to obey, made it too easy to go along with whatever he asked. Come to think of it, she didn't care that they were criminals.

Elijah kept checking her out. Callie flushed. She seldom shied away from male attention, but the intensity of Elijah's focus made her stomach churn. He looked at her like he could see inside her. Maybe he just thought she was hot and wanted to fuck her.

She tucked her hair behind her ears. Let him look at her. She had nothing to hide.

"You want to kiss me," said Elijah, sitting next to her.

Callie reddened and gaped at him. How did he know that?

"You do, don't you?" He raised an eyebrow. She blushed deeper. "Answer me, Callie."

The words sprang from her lips. "I do."

Elijah's grin widened. "I want to kiss you, too."

Callie's heart thudded. No one else moved as Elijah crept close to her, a golden vision in the firelight. She couldn't keep her eyes off him, couldn't look away, couldn't move—not even when he stopped in front of her.

"I bet you taste like sunshine." His voice was low, smooth, dangerous. It dizzied her.

"I might."

Elijah leaned in, hand cupping her cheek. Callie's eyes fell shut, and she met him halfway, mouths sliding together. Elijah's lips were hot, his kiss deliberate. His hand at the back of her neck urged her closer.

"Callie?" Ramsay asked. "What are you doing here?"

Callie broke the kiss with a gasp. Elijah pulled back. Ramsay had walked into the campground.

Jabari stood and kissed Ramsay. He slipped his arm around Ramsay's shoulders. Ramsay only had eyes for Callie.

Not knowing what else to do, she stood. "I could ask you the same thing."

"Jabari invited me. What's going on?" He scowled at Elijah, then looked to Callie. "Are you okay?"

She didn't know. Her mouth and cheeks burned, and she wanted to kiss Elijah again and nothing made sense anymore. She was in a strange place with strange people at a strange time of night, and she couldn't remember why she'd come back to the boardwalk.

"Callie," Ramsay said.

"Yeah, sorry. I'm fine." Shit, she had to focus. Maybe she'd forgotten to take her medicine again. Maybe that was the problem. She usually took it before she went to bed—

"It was consensual, if that's what you're worried about," said Elijah.

"I want to hear it from her," said Ramsay.

"I... yes, it was." Callie chewed her lip. "I wanted him to kiss me."

"Okay, weird. Whatever." Ramsay crossed his arms. "What are you doing here? You didn't drop by just to get your rocks off with... whoever this is."

"That's Elijah," said Jabari.

"I can introduce myself." Elijah stretched out a hand for Ramsay to shake. "Elijah. I'm in charge around here."

Ramsay ignored his hand. "You don't own me. Or her."

"I'm fine," Callie said. "Really, Ram. I promise."

"Have you met up with him before?" he asked. "Before tonight, I mean."

Callie shook her head. Her blush deepened. "I... well, we just met."

"An hour ago," Elijah added.

Ramsay's forehead creased. "You're making out with

some dude you just met? Callie, this isn't like you. What's going on?"

She wasn't sure why, but she felt like she needed to defend Elijah. "He's a nice guy, Ram. He hasn't done anything creepy, okay? He's been a gentleman, and he—"

"What's his last name?"

Callie gaped at him. "I... okay, what's Jabari's?"

Ramsay's face fell. "You know that's not fair."

"No. I don't know that." She put her hands on her hips. "As far as I can see, there's no difference, so back off. I can make my own decisions."

"Shitty ones," said Ramsay.

Callie's mouth tightened. What could she say to that? She didn't know why he was so pissed, but she didn't want to get into it with him now, especially not in front of this group of hot people. All she wanted to do was keep kissing Elijah, and Ramsay had impeded that. She had to get him out.

As if on cue, Jabari touched Ramsay's shoulder. "Why don't we go somewhere?"

Ramsay didn't move. "I'm comfortable here."

"I don't think you are, Ram. Come on." Jabari tugged on his arm, but Ramsay stood still, staring dead-eyed at Callie. Jabari tried again. "There's a club nearby. I think we all could go."

Elijah lit up. "Think we need a night out. Could do everyone a world of good."

Callie chewed the inside of her cheek. She still struggled to remember why she'd come to the boardwalk. Normally, it would have bothered her that she couldn't remember something that seemed so critical, but... being in the group's presence had calmed her. Nothing else mattered besides hanging out with them.

If she had to go to a club, maybe it wasn't the worst

thing. Besides, she could always come back to the board-walk once she remembered why she'd come there.

"Callie," said Elijah. "What do you think?"

What did she think? She was in over her head. Like, way in over her head. Her mind wasn't in the right place for her to decide. In all honesty, she felt tipsy, although she had had no alcohol. She was just drunk on Elijah.

The thought flipped her stomach and not in a good way. Callie swallowed.

"Might be fun," she offered weakly. "Haven't been to a club in a while. What do you think, Ram? I'm game if you are."

Something flashed in Ramsay's eyes. Callie couldn't place it. He put on a smile. "Yeah, why not? A club sounds fun. Jabari's been dying to teach me to dance."

Jabari grinned like he couldn't sense the tension, but Callie was sure he could—it would be impossible to ignore it. He whispered something in Ramsay's ear.

Callie wanted to roll her eyes, but she held back.

Elijah slipped his arm around her waist and pulled her against his side. His skin was hot even through his clothes. How would it feel against her bare skin?

She blushed again. Jesus. What was going on with her? She'd never felt so sensitive around a guy before. Maybe his cologne was messing with her head or something.

"Okay," said Elijah. "Let's head out to Indigo."

"We can't get in," Callie said. "The wait list is like six months out."

"Not for us." Maeve smiled. "Elijah handles it."

Callie looked at Elijah. She expected him to look smug, but he shied away from the attention. Maybe he was humble after all. Although... what favors did he have to call in, and what gave him pull over anyone outside the Starlight Boardwalk?

Then again, she had essentially just met him and already wanted to give him everything she had.

"Okay then," Callie said. "Let's go."

Part of her hoped Ramsay would object so they could go home and talk about this situation. But Ramsay still seemed mad at her, and she'd come to the boardwalk for... something. She still couldn't remember, and maybe that should have bothered her more, but it didn't. It was an unscratched itch at the back of her mind. Nothing more.

6

They ended up walking to Indigo. The summer night air was balmy, but Callie let Elijah hold her hand even though her palm was sweaty, and it was way too hot for physical contact. It felt nice, holding hands with someone again.

Elijah caught her eye, and he winked. Maybe she'd made the right choice. Elijah squeezed her hand and Callie smiled.

"Something the matter?" he asked.

She shook her head. "Just thinking. How much farther is it?"

"Not too much, darling. You don't mind walking, though. We'll get to know each other better."

How did he know her so well? Her feet had hurt before, but they didn't hurt now. She wasn't sure what had changed. Elijah had a point—it was a lovely night, and it was nice to talk to someone other than Ramsay for a change.

Parked cars lined the streets on either side of them as they walked. The pavement was uneven where tree roots had stretched too far, and Callie had to watch her step.

Downtown Neap Bay was all brick-sided buildings with colorful, tattered awnings. It was quaint.

Callie looked back over her shoulder. Ramsay and Jabari were holding hands too. Ramsay whispered something in Jabari's ear but pulled back when he made eye contact with Callie. She faced forward again, frowning. How had they let men come between them?

"Don't worry about them," Elijah urged. "Your brother's in a bad mood, but we can pull him out of it, right?"

Callie felt the heat of someone's gaze—someone other than Elijah's—and looked to their left. Maeve and Tahlia had been walking and talking together, but now Maeve had her attention on Callie, her eyes wide. Was it Callie's imagination, or did she look concerned? If she'd known Maeve better, maybe she would have asked about it. As it was, she looked away from Maeve and tried to return her attention to Elijah.

He stroked the back of her hand with his thumb. Her head hurt. Looking at Elijah made it worse somehow.

"I don't know if I feel up to clubbing," she admitted. "I don't like dancing, really."

"Sure, you do," he said. Pain flared in her forehead, and she winced. He kept going. "We won't stay all night, and you'll have fun. I promise."

A memory of Becca, sweaty and smiling, lurched to the front of her consciousness. *"Raves go all night, Cal. Gotta keep up."*

Becca. Callie froze. That was the reason she'd gone to the boardwalk. She'd gone looking for her lost bracelet.

Elijah halted with her. Ramsay and Jabari almost slammed into them, and Jabari swore. Tahlia and Maeve slowed to a stop and looked over.

"Darling," Elijah prompted.

"I have to go back," Callie said. "We—me and Ramsay—need to head back to the boardwalk."

"Like hell we do," said Ramsay. "I have everything I need."

But he didn't. He didn't have Callie, not anymore. If she told him she'd gone back for the bracelet, he would understand.

But she couldn't find the words. They were trapped inside somehow.

Elijah squeezed her hand again. She felt smothered, rather than comforted, by his nearness. She let go of his hand and stepped back.

"Callie," said Ramsay. "Don't be silly. Let's do this." It was the first time she'd heard softness in his voice. He wasn't holding Jabari's hand anymore, either. Maybe he really was worried about her. Maybe he cared. "Do you know how long it's been since I've gone out? I need it."

Or maybe he was thinking about himself again. Callie groaned and turned to Elijah. His eyes were still intense, but she wasn't frightened by him. He radiated safety, security, and peace.

Callie paused. A moment ago, she'd been wary of him, hadn't she? Now, she felt fine beside him. What had changed?

She'd looked into his eyes again. He'd convinced her somehow that he wasn't a threat by looking in her eyes. How had he done that? His eyes were so dark, so hungry. She needed to get close to him again. She had to. She—

"Cal," Ramsay said. "Are you listening to me?"

Callie nodded, though she felt worlds away from everyone. "Sure, we'll go to Indigo. But then... can we look for the bracelet?"

"We'll do whatever you want, darling, so long as you

agree to have fun." Elijah plastered a smile on his face again. Callie thought it wore thin at the edges. She wanted to believe he was being genuine, but something nagged at her. The more she looked at him, the more confused she felt. He kept talking as though he hadn't noticed her discomfort. "Tonight's about having fun, for all of us. My gang's been working hard, and you two could use a little break from life. Am I right?"

He couldn't know about Becca, could he? Beyond what she'd said about the bracelet, had she mentioned losing a sister? Callie racked her brain to remember all their conversations. She hadn't said a word about Becca. Elijah wasn't being specific, but his tone was pointed. It felt like he knew, and that was a feeling Callie couldn't shake. She shivered.

"Yeah. I mean, I could use a night out. We both could. It's been a while."

"It's settled then. Let's trudge onward," said Elijah.

He threaded his fingers through Callie's again, and she let him. What else could she do? It felt nice to hold his hand, and he kept reassuring her. She had some weird feelings about the situation, but maybe they had nothing to do with him.

She was so confused, it felt like she'd been drinking. Only she was stone-cold sober—in theory, anyway.

The amber glow of streetlamps made Elijah's cheeks look hollow, his expression ghoulish. Callie's stomach churned again.

They passed a backlit bar window with missing posters plastered to it. Callie didn't let her gaze linger on them for more than a few seconds. How had so many people disappeared from Neap Bay? There were more than she'd expected, most of them around her age.

A tabby cat darted out from a nearby alley and sprinted

across the street. Callie jumped and the whole group stopped to watch it run around the corner.

A slow smile spread across Elijah's face. He dropped Callie's hand and drifted over to Tahlia and Maeve. They spoke in hushed tones. Elijah pressed a kiss to Tahlia's cheek, and Callie suppressed a wave of jealousy.

Jabari let go of Ramsay's hand and shot Elijah a look. Elijah shook his head. Jabari looked like he wanted to say something. As he opened his mouth, Tahlia and Maeve drifted past him and followed the cat around the corner. Callie started after them.

"Wait," said Elijah.

"What are they doing?" Callie asked.

"Don't worry about it. They'll meet up with us at Indigo."

Callie's pulse quickened. Her head throbbed when Elijah spoke to her, and she wanted to listen to him, but she couldn't suppress her instincts for much longer. Something weird was happening. She couldn't understand why they'd all be so interested in a stray cat.

Before Elijah could stop her, she followed Tahlia and Maeve. She broke away from the group and ran.

"Callie," called Elijah.

But Callie kept running. She ran toward where they'd last seen the cat. Tahlia and Maeve must have chased it into another alley—Callie recognized the backs of their heads as she went around the corner. Her head had stopped hurting now that she was away from Elijah, but she didn't dwell on that.

The streetlight closest to the alley had a short, and it flickered as Callie passed it. She couldn't see the cat anymore. In the intermittent flashes of the streetlight, Maeve and Tahlia knelt beside a row of metal trashcans. All she could see was a dumpster—and to be honest, she smelled that one long before she saw it.

If the women heard her approach, they didn't react. It was hard for Callie to hear, but they were muttering to themselves. They must not have realized they'd been followed.

She'd almost made it to where the women were when the streetlight went out. Darkness swallowed the alley, and Callie's sight with it.

The tall buildings blocked out the moon, and she could barely see her hand in front of her face.

Callie pulled her cell phone out of her pocket. With trembling fingers, she switched on the flashlight. It glinted off the threads and beads in Tahlia's hair before the women's heads snapped up and turned toward Callie.

Callie staggered away from them like she'd been shot. Her brows knit together before rising into her hairline. Maeve and Tahlia gaped at her, revealing razor-sharp elongated canines. Their slitted pupils reflected the light like an animal's. Wet, bright blood coated their mouths, cheeks, and chins.

Callie dropped the phone, and it landed in a puddle. The flashlight went out. She wanted to scream, but no sound came. They were holding something too, just above the ground. She couldn't see what they were holding but she knew it was the cat, even before she saw its tail twitch in the dirt.

Maeve closed her mouth, but Tahlia hissed. It was a harsh, feral sound that Callie hoped she'd never hear again.

The women weren't women. They were monsters. Vampires, if she had to guess. But vampires didn't exist.

"Ramsay!" Callie screamed.

Elijah got there first. He vaulted over the hood of a

parked car and skidded into the alley. In two menacing strides, he was on Callie, breath hot on her face as he pinned her to the wall. His arms caged her in, and a knee between her legs kept her from ducking away.

Callie's gut heaved. She couldn't risk throwing up, couldn't move, couldn't do anything but stare wide-eyed at Elijah as he smiled at her. This time, he had the same fangs as his friends.

"Easy," said Elijah. "You don't want to ruin the game."

Callie tried to turn away from Elijah. He leaned in and she shut her eyes. Her pounding pulse drowned out all other sounds.

He pressed a kiss to her neck. The tip of his teeth grazed her skin, and she cried out. He broke away from her, wiping his mouth with the back of his hand.

"Careful, or I'll kill him," Elijah said softly.

Something slammed into the side of the parked car. Everyone looked up, including the women, who also let go of the cat.

"Can't see a thing," said Ramsay. "Jesus Christ. Callie?"

"Ramsay." Her voice was faint. Weak, like the call of a dying bird. She met Elijah's gaze. His mouth was closed, but he still smiled. She couldn't see his fangs but now she knew they were there. Why had she kissed him?

She didn't want him hurting Ramsay.

"Callie," Ramsay said again. He lingered at the end of the alley, peering into the darkness. "Shit, wait a second."

"You can't just explain this away," Callie told Elijah. "He'll figure it out."

"And what then?" asked Elijah. "What can he do about us?"

For the first time since he'd come into the alley, his tone chilled her. Until that point, he'd been as warm as he was at the boardwalk. Now the front was gone. He became less man, more monster. Still, he let her go.

Cold sweat slid down Callie's face. She shivered.

Ramsay was at her side in an instant. He took his phone out and shined its flashlight at her face. Her eyes slammed shut, and she raised a hand to shield her face.

"Warn somebody first, Ram."

"Jesus. You okay?"

"Yeah, I..." She looked to Elijah. He wasn't saying anything. She tried again. "I'm okay."

"What's everyone doing here?" Ramsay asked.

Jabari, who must have followed Ramsay over, kicked the streetlight at the end of the alley with his steel-toed boots. The light flickered and sprang to life again, illuminating the alley.

As he caught sight of Elijah, Callie, Tahlia, and Maeve, he only nodded, like it was normal.

They couldn't hide the blood. Ramsay was going to see it. He was going to figure it out, whether or not they wanted him to. Elijah would kill them.

Jabari spoke for everyone, as though he'd been there the whole time. "People leave drugs in this alley sometimes. That's what brought the girls here."

Ramsay quirked an eyebrow at the explanation. "Didn't know you guys did drugs."

Callie wanted to tell him that all of them were lying, that they were really a gang of bloodsucking monsters—but how would he ever believe that? The women had blood on them, but Ramsay didn't believe in vampires. Even if he knew the truth, what could he have done?

"You're pale, Cal," Ramsay said. "Did something happen? Are you hurt?"

"I'm fine," Callie said. "I just want to go home now. Elijah, it's been fun, but we're calling it a night."

"Why the rush, darling?" Elijah's smile was predatory, though his eyes were bright. Some part of Callie was still drawn to him, as though some unnatural thrall pulled them together, but he also terrified her.

She hadn't seen Jabari transform, had no proof he was a vampire or whatever the hell they were, but things were falling into place. His weird behavior after she'd fallen in the haunted house suddenly made sense. He wasn't squeamish or afraid of blood like they'd both speculated. It had entranced him. If she hadn't trusted her gut—if she'd somehow gone into his trailer with him alone, instead of going home with Ramsay, there was no telling how bad off she would be right now.

"Their faces." Ramsay gestured toward Maeve and Tahlia. "What's up with their faces?"

"Nosebleeds," Jabari said. "It's happened before. Must have snorted too hard."

Ramsay frowned, but he didn't contradict Jabari. He didn't know enough about drugs to argue. Neither did Callie. Even though she knew the truth, she couldn't prove it.

In her peripheral vision, Callie saw Tahlia open her purse, take out a pack of tissues and a bottle of water, and hand a tissue to Maeve. While the two of them cleaned their faces off, Elijah tossed Maeve a baggie. Callie couldn't see what was inside. She was mostly just floored that they'd done all those things without Ramsay seeing them.

"Let's not let one distraction make us veer off course," Elijah said. "Come on. Let's head out again."

"We want to go," said Callie.

"No, darling. You don't." He took Callie's hand and

tugged her after him. Like the other women, she followed. Something itched inside her head. Something she couldn't scratch.

She swallowed and steeled herself. "I don't want to go to the club anymore. I think Ramsay and I should go home."

Elijah tightened his hold on her. "What's the matter?"

Callie tensed. She kept her voice low, so only he could hear her. "Whatever you're doing to me, please stop."

"I don't know what you're talking about," he said.

"You've like... cast a spell on me or something, Elijah. I'm not stupid. I can feel it." She slipped out from beneath his arm, and he wrapped it around her waist instead, holding her hip so tight, it would bruise.

"I don't want to go to Indigo," Callie said. "You just made me feel that way. How much of tonight has been what you made up?"

His words came out in a hiss—still warm, but with the potential to sting. "I've only done a few things. The rest has all been us."

Callie scowled at him. She didn't try to get away from him. It seemed pointless. In fiction, vampires had super strength and super speed. Even if she broke free and started running, he was going to catch up with her. He was going to hurt her. So, what was the point?

"Did I even want to kiss you?" she asked.

Elijah groaned. "I only nudge free will a teeny bit. I can't create something from nothing."

Her heart skipped a beat. If what he said was true, she'd also wanted to go to Indigo, at least a little.

Whenever she thought about how she'd pictured sleeping with him, she felt dizzy. Lost. How could she believe a thing Elijah said?

She wanted to return to the boardwalk. She wanted to

look for Becca's bracelet, find it, and go home. She almost didn't give a shit whether Ramsay went back with her.

Surely if any of the vampires intended to hurt him, they would have done so already. He'd spent so much time alone with Jabari that anything else made no sense.

Then again, vampires made no sense. Not outside *True Blood*. They were fiction, right? Until that night, she never thought vampires existed. Now that she'd seen a group of them, she didn't know what to do next. Maybe real-life vampires had nothing in common with vampires in books and movies.

Were they going to kill her? Kill Ramsay? If so, why hadn't they done it already?

Callie's stomach heaved, but with nothing in it, she didn't puke. That didn't mean she didn't want to.

Elijah gripped her arm like a vise. "Keep walking and don't let him know what you've seen. If you do, you'll regret it. I promise you that."

Her head swam again. The more time she spent with Elijah, the less she felt like herself. Hadn't she read something about vampires being able to compel people? Maybe that was what Elijah was doing. She had no clue how to escape it, though. Maybe she couldn't escape it. Maybe she'd just have to keep fighting it as they went.

"I can be nice, too," Elijah said. "Please give me a reason to prove it."

Callie shivered. If Ramsay noticed something was off, he said nothing. He and Jabari coupled up again. They were even holding hands like nothing had changed.

She chewed the inside of her cheek. If she ruined Elijah's plan, he'd ruin her. Worse, he'd ruin Ramsay. She guessed she had to play along until they figured out his plan. Whatever the hell that was.

As they left the alley and resumed their walk, Indigo's spotlights cut through the clouds, moving in all directions. Callie heard the club before she saw it—throbbing bass, loud techno, the chatter of people waiting in line. It looked like the line wrapped around the building. No way they could get in without a connection.

Elijah tightened his hold on Callie's arm. She didn't resist. He was far too strong.

He leaned in close. "Let me do the talking, darling. I'll take care of everything."

Callie didn't doubt it. She was seriously regretting leaving her house. She couldn't remember the last time she'd gone out in the middle of the night, and she never wanted to again. Not with this crowd in tow.

She still couldn't believe vampires were real, let alone that she'd kissed one. All of this felt like a nightmare, or a fever dream she hadn't woken up from. She wished she could've gone home. She wished she'd never gone to the damn boardwalk.

Seemingly out of nowhere, Maeve came up to Elijah and Callie. Looking at her now, it was hard to remember the carnage she'd wrought in the alley, all the blood smeared on her face, her elongated canines. Now she was the same cool girl she'd always been to Callie. Somehow though, she seemed like less of a monster than Elijah did. Maybe because she hadn't done a thing to threaten Callie or Ramsay directly.

Maeve settled her hand on Elijah's shoulder. "Mind if I steal Callie?"

His eyes narrowed. He looked from her to Callie, then back again. "Only for a moment. Girl talk?"

"More or less."

Somehow, Callie doubted that. She wanted to argue that

she was fine where she was, but she sensed it would do her no good. If Maeve was a vampire like Elijah, she was as strong as he was too, which meant she could easily over-power Callie.

So, she nodded and tried to relax as Elijah passed her over.

Maeve lowered her voice as she pulled Callie to walk between her and Tahlia. Tahlia had said little since being the alley, and Callie wondered if she might have been embarrassed. She didn't know if feeding was a thing that embarrassed vampires.

"Don't talk to the bouncer or he'll kill you," Maeve whispered.

"The bouncer will?" Callie asked.

"No," said Tahlia. "Elijah."

Callie swallowed, holding her tongue. For now, she'd have to play along.

The line of people outside Indigo stretched around the corner. Callie doubted they could get in, but Elijah was smil-ing. As they moved past everyone else waiting to get into the club, the heat of their glares burned Callie. She kept her head down until they reached the bouncer.

The man by the door was tall and barrel-chested. His arms were the size of tree trunks. If he wanted to throw them out, he could easily do so.

"You can't skip the line," the bouncer said. "Who do you think you are?"

Elijah offered him a wicked grin. "You'll let us in no problem, friend."

The bouncer scrolled through an endless list on his tablet. He typed something in and waited. Then, he read the words that appeared onscreen, frowned, and cast a long, questioning look at Elijah.

Elijah nodded. "Go on."

"Of course, sir. My apologies." The bouncer wiped sweat from his brow. He looked around for a minute, still dazed, before lifting the black velvet rope for the group to step through. Several people behind them complained about the bouncer letting them in, but everyone ignored them, including Elijah and the bouncer.

The bouncer dipped his head. "Enjoy."

"I'm sure we will," Elijah said. His hand shot back, latched onto Callie's arm again, and dragged her to join him at the front of the group. Callie cast a helpless look back at Maeve, who only frowned at her, dejected.

As they wandered into the club, the noise level rose so much that Callie could barely hear herself think, let alone whatever Elijah was saying. His mouth was moving but it all just sounded like mumbling.

"What?" Callie shouted.

He raised his voice and tried again. "Would you like something to drink?"

The club was sprawling, massive. Ten times bigger than it looked outside, somehow. While Elijah kept busy at the bar, Maeve and Tahlia dragged Callie over to sit in a sunken lounge area with a table between them. The table was sticky from spilled drinks, and Callie wished she hadn't touched it. The couches they sat on were comfortable, if not cold. They must not have been used for a while, maybe because it was so late at night and most of the clubgoers were calling it quits if they hadn't headed out of there already.

The beads in Tahlia's hair clicked together as she leaned closer to Callie. Her voice was gentle. "He didn't hurt you, did he?"

"No. I think I'm fine." Callie rubbed her hip where he'd

held onto her. She'd have a bruise there too. "Is he always like that?"

"Elijah? No." Maeve shifted her position to get closer now that Tahlia had moved in. "He's usually more subtle. Turns the charm on for a while, couples it with compelling. I can tell he's been doing that one to you. Does your head hurt?"

"No," Callie said. "It did earlier, though. Hurts less when he's away but it doesn't disappear completely." Callie wasn't sure why they cared, so maybe it was time to just come right out and ask them.

"Why do you two care what happens to me? You're... you're all vampires, right? And you're *together*."

Tahlia hesitated, hand hovering above Callie's knee, before she let her fingers rest there. Her palm was cold and clammy.

"Elijah is dangerous," Tahlia said. "We know because we've seen everything he can do. When you're good, things are great. But... he's prone to mood swings. And once you irritate him, make him mad, whatever, there's no real going back."

"He can hurt you," Maeve added. "At first, we thought he wanted to play with you. Maybe feed on you later. Now... we're not so sure."

At the mention of feeding, Callie thought about the cat. She tried to suppress the memory of the part that came next, Tahlia and Maeve chasing it into the alley. "Is that why you two... with the cat? You needed to feed?"

"That's right," Tahlia said. "We were both weak."

"But what about Ramsay and me? Couldn't you have fed on us?"

"We could have, yes. But it wouldn't have been right. It would have gone against everything Maeve and I try to do."

Maeve nodded. "We're only half-vampires. Not full-fledged. Not like the others."

Callie's brow furrowed. "I don't follow."

"It's... a little complicated," Tahlia admitted. "This isn't the best place to explain. Basically, though, don't worry about us. We don't feed on humans."

"That's the crux, at least," Maeve said.

Callie had heard of vampires not turning fully until they an initiation. In *The Lost Boys*, anyone who'd started turning could stop the process if they didn't drink human blood and if they killed the vampire who sired them.

"You're not in your twenties, either," said Callie.

Maeve and Tahlia looked at each other. A slow smile spread across Tahlia's face. "No. We were once."

"Now, forever." Maeve winked. "We were lucky to turn when we did."

"We're in our late twenties," Tahlia said. "Been vamps since the eighties. We're not full-fledged, either. It's a pain in the ass."

"Like being vegetarian or vegan," Maeve said. "You know it's the right thing, but damn if that meat doesn't smell delicious."

Callie thought back to the alley, Elijah's mouth on her neck, teeth dragging over her flesh. A lump rose in her throat, and she swallowed. He'd wanted to bite her then. He could've killed her. But he hadn't.

"So, you... what?" Callie asked. "Don't drink human blood, but anything else is fair game?"

"Pretty much." Maeve flipped her hair over her shoulder. "Hence, the alley cat. Not our finest moment, and Elijah wouldn't have wanted you to see us feeding, but it was bad. We had to do it."

"Too long and we dry out," Tahlia said. "That's the only way we can 'die.'"

"We're undead, you know?" Maeve flagged down a cocktail waitress carrying a tray full of plastic cups. She smiled at the girl. "You'll give us three shots and leave, thanks."

The waitress tucked a strand of hair behind her ear. Then, she set the drinks on the table and headed back into the crowd without speaking.

"You compelled her," Callie said.

"It's helpful," Tahlia said. "Maeve does it more often than she needs to. I don't know how when it's so exhausting. Wears me out just watching."

"I don't feel any different, though," Callie said. "No headache or anything. When Elijah compelled the bouncer, I didn't feel too bad, either."

"Oh," Maeve said. "That's not how that works. You can only compel one person at a time. It takes concentrated energy. You weren't the target, so nothing happened to you."

"So, when I feel bad around Elijah, he wants that to happen?" asked Callie. "To me, specifically?"

"Unfortunately," Tahlia said.

They took the shots. As soon as the vodka hit the back of Callie's throat, she had to fight the urge to gag. Fatigue washed over her.

"I might head out," Callie said. "I'm tired."

"I want to dance," said Tahlia.

Maeve's eyes flashed. She grabbed Callie's hand and dragged them both to their feet. "You should dance with me."

Callie wasn't sure what to do. She let Maeve lead her away from the lounge and onto an open spot to dance. Tahlia followed them. Truth be told, Callie had never been a dancer. She wasn't looking forward to making a fool of herself in front of two hot women. Her mouth felt dry, like she had had nothing to drink in years. It was kind of hard to breathe. Callie hadn't felt like this around a woman in ages, and she wasn't sure how to feel about it now.

Maeve wasn't just a woman. She was a vampire. She could snap Callie in half and drain her dry if she wanted, like she had the cat.

Focus on the present, Callie thought, *or whatever. Get out of your head.*

The bass throbbed through Callie's body. Maeve gripped her fingers tightly as she led her through the crowd. People parted for them as they passed like they owned the dance floor. Callie looked ahead at Maeve, so sure of where she was going. She looked down at their hands. Maeve's sleeve had ridden up—

Callie jerked Maeve to a stop. She slid her hand up to wrap around Maeve's wrist. They froze there, standing and staring at each other.

There was a bracelet on Maeve's wrist, made of red and yellow threads woven carefully together. A silver charm hung from the center, one third of a friendship necklace. She'd recognize it anywhere.

No way, Callie thought.

"What the hell?" She lifted Maeve's arm and held it up between them to get a better look at the bracelet.

Maeve hesitated before handing it over. "I was going to tell you. I promise."

Callie's face fell. "Have you had it the whole time?"

"I..." she looked to Tahlia, whose lips pressed together in a thin line. Tahlia shook her head, frowning. Maeve tried again. "You didn't drop this, Callie. Jabari took it from you."

"What?" Callie secured the bracelet on her wrist. Jabari

hadn't even touched her. "No, he couldn't have. I would have seen or felt something."

"We're all pickpockets," Tahlia said. "Light fingers. He snatched it off your wrist while you were talking to Ramsay."

"You knew I was looking for it, Maeve. Why didn't you say something earlier? You even asked me about it."

"Elijah said we couldn't. He didn't... he wanted to meet you, Callie. If we said anything and ruined his chances, he—"

Callie turned without waiting for Maeve to finish. Nothing she could say would improve the situation. As she pushed through the crowd, she couldn't help feeling over-whelmed. The more time she spent with this gang, the more lies she uncovered. What would come next?

Callie passed Ramsay and Jabari. They danced close, cheek to cheek, and Callie wanted to scream. Ramsay had no clue what he'd gotten himself into. But if she tried to warn him, Elijah would—

Elijah. Callie was so busy looking at Ramsay that she didn't see him and slammed into Elijah's chest instead. He held two drinks aloft, trying to keep from spilling them.

"Callie." Even just her name was a threat on his lips. "Wondered where you'd run off to. Let's chat."

It wasn't a question. Callie's pounding head said he was trying to compel her. She needed to ask Tahlia and Maeve how to fight that.

"You stole my bracelet," she said.

"Not me, darling. Jabari." Elijah proceeded like it was no big deal. He offered Callie a cup filled with something dark. "I figured red wine was a safe enough choice. You drink, don't you? Tell me."

"I... do." Callie's voice came out smaller than she'd

intended. Almost without thinking, she took the cup from Elijah. He raised his own to hers in a toast.

"To getting along," he said. "You'll only get the truth now."

Callie held the cup to her lips, met Elijah's eyes, and drank.

7

The wine was metallic, backed with iron—no, copper. It had to be copper. Who had decided to serve it in a Moscow Mule cup? She'd seen no one do that before. The aftertaste was heavy, sweet with a kick of spice. Was it cinnamon or something?

"How's the house blend?" Elijah asks.

"Tastes like shit," said Callie. "I would have preferred a beer."

"Never took you for a beer girl."

"Yeah? Well, now you know."

It was too easy to forget she was mad at Elijah, and a little terrified of him. With him so close to her, and how good he looked and smelled, it was too easy to give him whatever he wanted.

Callie didn't know how much of her was being compelled, or how much was her free will. She remembered what he'd said before.

"I only nudge free will a teeny bit. I can't create something from nothing."

He tipped his drink toward her, offering it. "I went with whiskey, straight. You're welcome to try it."

"No, thank you." She made a face and tried to push past Elijah, but his hand on her shoulder stopped her.

"Callie." His voice was low, like it had been when he'd cornered her in the alley, but smoother. Gentler. His tone was imploring. "You're still freaking out about what you saw. About... us being vampires. You're one of the few people in Neap Bay who knows the truth."

The music changed, and the dance floor glowed. Everyone dancing cheered. The DJ sat on a platform above them, yelling something she couldn't make out. Callie's head buzzed.

"I would have preferred to remain anonymous, to lie low here for a while, but I worry it's no longer possible," Elijah continued. "Can I trust you to be discreet, darling? I'd hate for you to worry Ramsay unnecessarily." He looked toward her brother, who was still dancing with Jabari. "Besides, we're not hurting anyone. You saw Maeve and Tahlia with the cat. We don't even need to feed on humans."

The gears turned in Callie's head. She wanted to believe him. Her head no longer hurt, which meant he wasn't trying to compel her. He was just... what? Trying to have a heart-to-heart with her? How could he do that when his heart wasn't beating?

God, but he was gorgeous. She couldn't think straight even without him compelling her.

His reassurances rang hollow in her ears. As she racked her brain to figure out why, Callie remembered what Maeve had told her about the gang's status.

"We're only half-vampires. Not full-fledged. Not like the others."

"Wait," Callie said. "What are you and Jabari?"

"What do you mean?" asked Elijah.

"Maeve and Tahlia, they said they don't feed on people. But they said you and he were full-blooded, which means you feed on... more than cats, right?" Her brow furrowed. "Humans, then? You make meals out of people?"

"You put it too simply." He sounded more amused with her than frustrated, and that got under Callie's skin. She didn't like to think that she only entertained him.

"But that's it, isn't it?"

"Yes. It is." His eyes darkened as he took a step toward her. Callie stepped back. He smirked. "You're afraid of me now."

"Why shouldn't I be?" She still felt hurt by him, but she tried to keep that out of her voice. She hated admitting he had the upper hand, but it was worse for her to let him know he'd upset her at the boardwalk. That was before she'd even known he was a vampire. Somehow, being hurt by "human" Elijah had been worse.

Probably because she'd let no one she'd kissed get that close to her feelings. It was more intimate than it should have been. Callie was usually quick about shutting that shit down. It was better not to get attached. She'd learned that after her father had walked out on them all those years ago. All the good ones left.

She fought hard against the memory of his departure, of herself as a girl with braided pigtails, sobbing with her siblings as her mother let them know he was never coming back. That he no longer loved them.

"You've given me no reason to hurt you, Callie. You're far more valuable alive to me than dead. I suppose I could turn you if you asked nicely, though." He winked. "Or sweetened the deal with something else."

She was more than a little offended. Maybe offering to

turn her was a gesture of goodwill, but it only made her more anxious.

"I don't want to turn, Elijah."

"Then I don't have to turn you. I'll just feed on you."

Callie tore away from Elijah. He sneered but didn't follow. She made her way through the crowd to Ramsay and Jabari grinding on the dance floor.

"Ram," she said. "We need to talk."

He groaned and stepped away from Jabari. Jabari left his hands on Ramsay's shoulders. Callie's frustration flared again.

"What's wrong now?" Ramsay asked.

"We need to get out of here. Maeve has the bracelet. I was going to dance with her and then I saw it on her wrist. Apparently, Jabari stole it—"

"The hell I did," Jabari said. "Don't bring me into this."

Callie had a feeling he was lying so he could look good in front of Ramsay. There was no point in arguing. At least she knew the truth.

"I have it and I'm going home. Come with me." Callie reached up and rubbed the back of her neck. The men were just staring at her. "Ramsay? Did you hear me?"

"What are you talking about?" he asked. "I thought you had to go get Becca's bracelet."

"I just told you, I have it, you know what? Never mind. You clearly don't give a shit what I say right now." Callie was fuming. She needed to stop talking before she said something she'd regret, but the words were coming out too fast. "You're stuck so far up Jabari's ass, it's a wonder you can breathe."

Ramsay's eyes narrowed, and he scoffed. For a moment, he said nothing. Right as Callie thought their conversation was finished, he opened his mouth again.

"You're cramping my style. Serious bad vibes here, Cal. Also, you need to make up your damn mind who you want tonight. Watching you go back and forth is exhausting." Ramsay inhaled loudly, like taking Callie down a peg had winded him. "Or hell, have a threesome with them. I don't care. Just please, leave us alone."

Callie gaped at him. She and Ramsay had fought before, but he'd never been this rude. It was an attitude he never would have showcased with Becca living. She almost reminded him of that. Almost. But the pain of Becca's memory was too much for her, and Callie had hurt enough for one night.

"I'm going home," she said again. "Come with me now, or don't. I don't care. But I'm not covering for you with Mom."

"Fine by me. Later, bitch."

The epithet pricked Callie's eyes with tears. She didn't dare shed them where Jabari could see. She didn't want Ramsay to know he'd hurt her, either. What had gotten into him? Jabari made him act so much unlike himself. Could it be that he was compelling him?

Becca never would have called her a bitch. Not even as a joke.

Callie yearned for her sister. The pain was so profound, she had to look away from Ramsay. Maeve and Tahlia were dancing where Callie had left them. They swung their hips and held each other. Their closeness made Callie blush. Maybe it was better not to get involved. It wasn't too late to leave.

But then, Maeve lifted her gaze from Tahlia so her eyes landed squarely on Callie. A jolt went through Callie at the look, one not altogether bad. Maeve must have sensed it somehow because she smirked. *Damn it,* Callie thought. *Now she knows she has me cornered.*

She wasn't sure why it bothered her so much anymore, either. Maybe it didn't.

When Tahlia realized someone else had snagged Maeve's attention, she turned to look at Callie too. Then, she and Maeve exchanged a knowing look. Tahlia winked at Callie before slinking away to talk to Elijah or someone else, Callie didn't even care anymore. Maeve turned toward Callie with that same easy smirk on her face and swing in her step, and Callie knew she was a goner.

"Dance with me," Maeve said. "Before you go, I mean. I won't compel you. Please."

"Did you compel me last time?" asked Callie.

Maeve frowned but didn't answer. She held a hand out to Callie. Her palm looked soft, her nails were short, painted black, and chipped. Callie wasn't sure why she hadn't run away yet.

"Please," Maeve said. "It's just a dance. I know you don't know me, but... I'm not Elijah. I don't threaten people for no reason, and I certainly don't go after someone I just met."

The implication made Callie blush.

Maeve's hands settled on Callie's hips. Callie put her hands on Maeve's shoulders. The song changed to something evocative. Moody and bass heavy. Callie and Maeve locked eyes, and Maeve winked.

"Not gonna have to teach you to dance now, am I?"

"N-no." Callie wasn't sure why she'd stammered. Was she nervous? Jesus. Maeve was hot. Callie tried again. "I'm a decent dancer."

"Show me."

Maeve kept eye contact with Callie while she slid her

hands around to Callie's lower back. Everywhere she touched, she left fire in her wake.

The music throbbed and flowed around them. The longer and the closer they danced, the more Callie felt like they were the only people in the club.

As Maeve pulled Callie closer, Callie arched into her touch. She couldn't help it. Although she didn't think Maeve was compelling her, she put her at ease. While Callie's heart fluttered in her chest, it wasn't from fear, but excitement.

They swung their hips to the music. Callie tried to let loose, relax, have fun—but she was all too aware of the heat between them as their bodies pressed together and moved in sync. It was too easy to imagine how they'd fit together. Too easy for Callie to let her imagination run away with her.

Maeve's breath warmed Callie's lips. She smelled like cinnamon. It would have been too easy for Callie to close the distance between them and kiss her. If she just leaned forward...

"I have to go," said Callie. "Now, or I'll regret it."

She sprinted across the dance floor. People cursed as she shoved them out of the way. Callie didn't stop to look back over her shoulder, to ponder the hurt in Maeve's eyes as she'd pulled away from her. All she thought about was that she had to get back home.

For a moment, she felt guilty. She'd left Ramsay in there, alone, surrounded by vampires. Of course, he didn't know they were vampires, which only made everything worse. But... the way he'd gone off on her in there, maybe he just needed some space. Surely if Jabari had wanted to hurt him, he would have done it already.

Part of her didn't care if something *happened* to Ramsay. Not after how he'd spoken to her.

Callie made a mental note to text her brother, just as

soon as she got somewhere safe. Even if he didn't understand why she'd run off, at least he'd know she'd made it home safely.

By the time Callie burst through the remaining clubgoers and into the open air again, cold sweat chilled her skin. The summer breeze lifted the hair off her neck but did next to nothing to soothe her frayed nerves. She'd wandered into an alley rather than outside the front of the club as she'd hoped. She had to find somewhere to hide, and fast.

Her eyes fell on a dumpster surrounded by trash bags. The dumpster was too conspicuous, and too disgusting, but maybe she could crouch and hide behind the bags? The shadows were deep enough. If she didn't move, maybe—

Movement in the doorway stole her attention. She had to go, now, consequences be damned. Callie ran over and got down behind the trash bags. The smell was undeniable, but she breathed through her mouth as quietly as she could and kept her back pressed to the wall.

Callie waited. Maeve drifted out of the club, presumably looking for her. Maybe the bracelet too because the vampires still needed leverage against her. Callie was almost surprised she'd held herself back. Tahlia and Elijah followed her. From her limited vantage point, Elijah didn't look too worried. Shouldn't he have been more concerned about her running off and telling someone what she'd seen?

"Callie," Maeve said. "Are you okay? Are you out here?"

"Callie," Elijah echoed. His voice held a warning Callie didn't care to consider. Had he told the other vamps his intentions for her? Did he really want to kill her or turn her or what?

Maybe it was better not to think about Elijah. Instead, she thought about Maeve.

The vampires continued to call out for her, but Callie

stayed hidden, pressed to the wall. She didn't know if their superhuman senses or whatever would let them pick her up if she wasn't moving, but it was worth a shot. She closed her eyes, too, like somehow if she couldn't see them, they couldn't see her. Again, it was worth a shot.

Her heart climbed into her throat. How long before they gave up on her?

"Don't think she's out here," Tahlia said. Callie couldn't see who she was talking to. Why did any of them care that she'd left?

"I might have scared her off," Maeve said. Callie felt an odd twinge at her words—no, make that her tone. She sounded almost sad about it. Regretful.

Maybe Maeve did like Callie after all.

Why did Callie care?

"Shit," Elijah said. "Well, what can you do? The night's still young. Let's go get into some trouble."

Callie kept her eyes closed. She held her breath. She waited.

After a minute, the crunch of shoes on cobblestones stopped. Callie exhaled and opened her eyes. She pushed away from the wall to peek past the trash bags.

Everyone had left the alley. She was alone again.

Callie felt a little sad about how she'd left things with Maeve, but she was a goddamn vampire. And she'd lied to Callie.

She waited for another minute to make sure the vampires weren't coming back. Then, she fired off a text to Ramsay, explaining where she'd gone. Callie stood and headed out of the alley, down the street, and back to the boardwalk.

Indigo's throbbing bass, coupled with the scent of Maeve's perfume, followed her all the way back.

8

The next day, light streaming through the blinds jerked Callie awake. A patch of sunlight burned her closed eyelids. She recoiled, backing against her pillows to away from the sun's assault.

What time was it?

She checked her smartwatch. Three o'clock in the afternoon.

Panic slammed into her chest. Had Ramsay made it back?

The heat of the midday sun along with its brightness should have let her know she'd slept so late. Her mouth felt stuffed with cotton. Then again, so did her heart. She shifted to the edge of the bed and winced when the movement made her forehead throb.

It felt like a hangover, but she'd only had some wine. Could it be that she'd overdone it emotionally or something instead? Maybe it was just from Elijah compelling her so much. A vampire magic hangover, or whatever. It didn't matter. Whatever had happened to Callie, she'd woken up feeling like shit. She would never drink again.

Callie stiffened and snatched her cell phone off the nightstand. Thankfully, she'd plugged it in before going to bed the night before. Once she'd unlocked the phone, she navigated to her messages. There were more than she expected, and not just from Ramsay. She tackled the ones from him first.

Callie swiped into one of his messages and read:

Callie where tf are you?

Shit, had her message to him not gone through? She had texted him, hadn't she? Callie scrolled up—yes, her hasty message to Ramsay before leaving Indigo was there. Maybe he'd been too preoccupied to see it. Callie frowned and read his next message, sent fifteen minutes later:

lol I'm out of it, just saw you went home. Might be tipsy idk. bummerrrrr. did you get the bracelet at least?

And there were two more messages in the thread, both of which triggered all kinds of emotions:

Elijah and Maeve asked for your number. I gave it to them. hope that's good

And:

Sorry for calling you a bitch at Indigo. I'll be with J. love ya

Callie's heart throttled her ribcage. If the vampires hadn't killed Ramsay, she was sure as shit going to. Why did he think it was okay to give her number to Maeve, let alone Elijah? He wasn't the sharpest knife in the block, but surely even he could tell that something was fucked up, that the tension between her and Elijah had increased as the night progressed, and not in a good way. And then, there was Maeve. She'd told Ramsay about Maeve to his face, explained she'd lied about the bracelet. So why was Ramsay acting like they were all a group of friends?

An ache spread through Callie's temple into her eye socket. She pressed the heel of her hand against her closed eye, but the pain only intensified. Shit, maybe that wine had been a lot stronger than she'd thought.

Fear replaced the pain. What if Elijah had put blood in it?

True to Ramsay's word, she had messages from two unsaved numbers that she didn't recognize. Callie's finger hovered over the first one, and she fought to keep the tremor from her hand as she tapped it.

Sorry about your bracelet. It was all a mess. It's fucked. I'd love for you to hear me out.

Hang on a minute. That one had to be Maeve, right? It sure didn't sound like Elijah. Callie chewed the inside of her cheek and opened the other message. This one was shorter, but it raised the hairs on the nape of her neck.

Be careful, darling.

Bile burned the back of her throat. That one had to be Elijah. He was the only one who called her *darling*, and there was no mistaking the threat in the text, even though it was short. When he was around, he made her anxious, but he also thrilled her in the most delicious way. Stripped of proximity, he was only terrifying. Just thinking about him made her want to throw up.

Callie tapped back to Ramsay's messages. Was Elijah's message a warning, or a declaration? Could it have been an admission of guilt? Maybe he'd done something to Ramsay after she'd left. Maybe he—

Shit. She had to call Ramsay.

The cell phone rang twice, then went to voicemail. The sound of his voice flipped her stomach. She would've given anything to know he was all right.

Callie ended the call and sent him a text:

Hope you're with Jabari. Please let me know when you get this. I'm worried

Even if he thought she was overreacting, what difference did it make? She wouldn't apologize for wanting to know whether he was still alive. After all, he hadn't seen what she had. Hell, he didn't even know they were vampires at all, unless they'd shown him their true colors after she left.

Callie took a deep breath and tried to center herself. All she could do now was wait for his response.

She tapped back to what she assumed was Maeve's message. It seemed like she wanted to patch things up. She wanted Callie to hear her out. She'd acknowledged the weirdness of the situation. Maybe it was worth a shot to talk to her.

Callie waited a minute before typing her message:

Last night was weird. Assuming this is Maeve. Can we meet somewhere to talk? Like, away from Elijah and the others?

The ball was in the vampire's court now. Callie wiped

her sweaty palms on her pajama pants. Whatever came next, at least she'd tried.

She was just about to delete Elijah's message when Maeve texted her back:

Definitely don't want him there either. Love to meet up. Has to be after sundown for obvious reasons.

Callie frowned and replied:

So the sunlight thing isn't a myth?

She set her phone aside, changed into regular clothes, and looked at herself in the mirror. She was fixing her tousled hair when the phone chimed again. Maeve had texted her:

Yes and no. We don't explode it the sun but standing in it feels like the worst rash or allergic reaction you've ever had. Not great

That made sense to Callie. It sucked, though. She never thought she would've taken walking in the sun for granted. She still knew so little about vampires, and everything she knew came from movies, books, television, and video games. How much of it was true?

She couldn't say she trusted Maeve. She didn't trust any of the vampires. Maeve might not give her a straight answer if she asked, but hell, she had to do something. Maybe she could get answers from Maeve to use against Elijah.

Hesitantly, Callie fired off another text:

Garlic? You can't eat garlic or get anywhere near it, right?

Callie swore she heard Maeve's laughter in her response:

You think we'd have eternal life only to be defeated by a spice? No way. Although we have a general distaste for it, so no Italian dinners in my future

Callie smirked. She tapped her fingernails against the side of the phone before she responded:

So sad. I think I would die without pasta. Anyway, what about holy water? Or crosses? Does that shit hurt you or??

Callie wondered if Maeve was tiring of her yet. She tried to picture what she could be doing. Was she in her trailer now? Was she anywhere near Elijah? Or was she lying in bed? Callie tried to picture the inside of Maeve's trailer and failed. Maybe she was with Tahlia. The two of them seemed cozy with Elijah. Maybe they were hooking up. She didn't know what to think anymore. The previous day, she hadn't thought vampires were real. Last night, she'd kissed one.

Jesus. The memory made anxiety roil in Callie's gut.

Maeve texted back, just in the nick of time:

Holy water is awful. Like, the Worst. Crosses aren't cool, but they do nothing. They're just kind of offensive, you know?

Callie was about to text back when another came through:

But enough about me. You want to talk about last night?

Callie gulped. And there it was. She'd assumed that meeting up with Maeve would provide her with answers about Elijah and the gang, but she hadn't expected to give up anything in return. Maeve had lied to her, but she hadn't seemed threatening toward Callie. She hadn't cornered her and tried to bite her, like Elijah. And she hadn't threatened Ramsay. If she had any shot at making friends or allies with the vampires, Maeve was her best bet. Maybe Tahlia too, although Callie didn't know her well enough yet.

Maeve wanted to know why she'd run last night. She could say it had everything to do with the bracelet, but they both knew that wasn't the issue. Nor had Elijah's threat fully terrified her. No, what had really freaked Callie out was her budding attraction toward Maeve. She'd been hot and somewhat heavy with Elijah, though now she assumed a great deal of that had been his idea. Maeve had sworn she wasn't compelling Callie, and Callie hadn't gotten a headache like she had with Elijah.

Which meant that Callie was at least a little into her.

What would've happened if she hadn't run off? If they'd kept dancing? If they had kissed?

Callie braced a hand against her stomach to fight the butterflies. How long had it been since she'd felt so conflicted about someone? Maeve wasn't Elijah, but she was dangerous. Ignoring everything else, she was a vampire. Callie couldn't deny how terrified and shocked she'd been in the alley. Seeing Maeve hunched over the cat like that, teeth and face slicked with blood... it wasn't a sight she could dismiss, let alone forget.

She'd never believed in the paranormal, not even ghosts. At Becca's funeral, some people had tried to console her with affirmations on the afterlife, but Callie had never believed in that either. You only got one life, and then that was it. You had to make your time on earth count. Maybe that was why accepting Becca's death had been so difficult.

Callie's fingers fumbled over the screen as she replied to Maeve:

We can meet up at dark, around 9 tonight. Gemstone Diner. Does that work for you?

She glanced toward the mirror again. Before she went anywhere, she needed to not only do some soul-searching, but take care of her hair. And put on some makeup. And maybe some nice clothes. Gemstone wasn't swanky, but there would be people around. Plus, the fries were incredible.

Shit, she thought, *it's not a date.* But maybe it was. Maybe a little.

Anxiety squeezed her intestines. What if she was walking into a trap? What if Elijah was the one texting her, or worse, what if he pulled Maeve's strings and had gotten her to go along with him? She still knew next to nothing about their relationship. Maybe they'd unite to kill her or whatever. Maybe that had been the plan from the beginning.

No, that couldn't be the case. Callie refused to believe that.

Maeve's reply came faster than Callie had expected, and her chest constricted as she read it:

If that's not past your bedtime, that's perfect for me

Callie looked at the phone again and fired off a message before she talked herself out of the whole situation:

Great. See you then

Just as she sent the text, her phone buzzed again. Ramsay was calling. She hit the green button.

"Hey, you all right?"

"Just peachy, thanks. I'm with Jabari. I stayed the night with him. You know, like I told you." She could feel his frustration, but it wasn't worth a fight. He didn't know what all she'd been through, and if he was safe, that was all she really cared about. "Callie? You there?"

"Shit, Ram, sorry." Pain spiked in the front of her forehead again. "I think I'm hungover or something. It sucks."

"Me too," Ramsay said. "But I think I had more than you did. Jabari gave me some wine and it—"

"You never drink wine."

"I made an exception. It was bougie as hell. Had to be older than 1920 or something, I don't really remember. Not bad, all things considered." There was rustling on the other end of the phone, like he was sitting up in bed or something. "I don't know how, but it seems like Elijah is loaded. Maybe he's old money."

"I don't think they really work for the boardwalk," said Callie.

"Is that what they told you?" Ramsay scoffed. "No way. As far as I know, they're drifters, but they've been in Neap Bay for a while. Jabari steals. I bet the others do too."

Callie's brow furrowed. "How do you know he steals?"

"Because I saw him, obvi. Last night at Indigo, he took some lady's wallet."

Callie groaned. Ramsay tended to not only fall in with the wrong crowd, but to fall in love with it too. If Jabari was stealing, along with the rest of the group, it was only a matter of time before Ramsay joined them. So far, he'd only gotten a few speeding tickets. He didn't need a criminal record.

"What?" Ramsay asked.

"I don't like you hanging out with him. You know that." She dragged a hand over her face. "He still gives me the creeps, and he—"

"I don't want to hear it, Cal." Ramsay muttered something under his breath. Then, he continued, "Why can't you be happy for me?"

"I am happy for you, Ram. I'm just worried. You barely know Jabari, and he... well, the group he runs with isn't great."

She searched for the best words. She couldn't come out and say that they were vampires, could she? He'd never believe her. He didn't believe in vampires, although he believed in ghosts. She could play the concerned sister all she wanted, but she wasn't getting through to him.

"Becca would worry too," Callie tried.

There was a long pause on the other end. Had the call disconnected. "Ram?"

"Yeah. Still here." He exhaled loudly into the receiver. "Look, you're feeling weird and shitty, and I don't really want to talk about this anymore. I was calling you as a favor. Now I wish I hadn't."

"Come on, don't be like th—"

"Bye, Callie."

"Ramsay—"

Click. He'd hung up. Callie lowered the phone from her ear and set it in her lap. She stared down at the blank screen. More than anything, she felt like crying. All she could do was keep moving, and right now that meant meeting Maeve.

She texted Ramsay, *sorry,* and then jumped in the shower. Maybe she wasn't sorry at all, but she had to smooth things over.

9

After almost fainting in the shower, blasting her hype playlist, and giving herself a pep talk, Callie pulled herself together enough to leave the house. She wore a denim skirt and a *Silence of the Lambs* T-shirt and had put on makeup and everything. Hangover or not, she wasn't about to look like shit in front of Maeve. If nothing else, if Maeve or Elijah killed her, she wanted to leave a pretty corpse.

Fucking morbid, Cals, Becca chided in her head. Callie felt like throwing up again, but she kept herself in check. No more setbacks. No time.

Sorry, Becca, Callie thought. *I can only disappoint one sibling at a time.*

Callie had always been the morbid one. She'd grossed the others out. At one point, she'd wanted to become a mortician, but in the wake of Becca's death, that interest had dried up. Now, she wanted a job that got her as far away from death—and pain—as possible.

Maeve had texted her once more to make sure she was coming. Like she even had a choice. There was no one else to go to. She didn't trust Elijah or any of the others, not even Tahlia, because she didn't know them well enough—or knew them *too* well, in Elijah's case.

Callie didn't want to text her back. She couldn't think of anything to say that wouldn't be better in person. Besides, as she reminded herself on the drive over to Gemstone Diner, if she gave Maeve too much insight into what she was thinking, she could use it against her.

But the odds of it being a trap had to be low, right? Especially since Maeve was letting Callie know about Elijah. That part, at least, didn't feel like a setup.

The Gemstone Diner was one of the closest restaurants to Callie's house. It felt like a massive tourist trap, which was weird for Neap Bay. It didn't attract many tourists. The diner could almost pass for a regular greasy-spoon joint, were it not for the enormous, illuminated sign above it that spelled out GEMSTONE in fake amethyst letters. Faux crystals and gems also lined the roof and random patches in the sides of the building. Inside, the 1950s decor boasted purple-and-white padded benches, tile floors, and tacky amethyst wall sconces. The only music the diner seemed to play was Enya, one of Susan's favorite artists, but Callie had no clue why.

The biggest draw of the Gemstone, for Callie, was that it was always packed, even late at night. Maybe not with tourists as the owners had intended, but with locals who enjoyed a good milkshake, a cheap burger, and the only vegan-friendly meat and dairy substitutes in town. Callie and Maeve weren't vegans—especially not Maeve, obviously —but everything else helped them. And if the place was full of people, maybe Maeve wouldn't feel like killing her.

Of course, Maeve didn't seem the type who didn't want to make a scene. If she—and Elijah—really wanted Callie dead, Callie knew they'd make it happen.

Still, she felt about as safe as she could, all things considered, when she pulled into the crowded parking lot. She looked around for Maeve's car before she remembered she didn't have one. She'd probably planned to walk to the diner, and Callie felt guilty that she hadn't considered the location's proximity to the boardwalk.

As she pushed through the front door, the hostess looked up from her podium and beamed at Callie. "How many in your party?"

"Just two."

"Sit wherever you want, and someone will be right with you."

Callie did as the hostess told her, choosing a booth with clean seats, a clean table, and an excellent view of the door. A waitress going into the kitchen noticed Callie, and they made eye contact before she held up a "one minute" finger. Callie nodded and checked her phone:

I see you.

She'd saved that contact as Maeve, not Elijah, but her heart still skipped a beat. What if she'd been wrong? Her phone buzzed again:

Kidding. I'm outside. You get us a table already?

Callie's shoulders relaxed. She sent a reply right away:

Yeah it's all good. Come on in

Not a minute later, Maeve breezed through the front door of the diner. She looked tousled, but still beautiful. It took Callie aback. A different septum ring glinted in her nose, but she was too far away for Callie to tell what it was. She wore a leather jacket, cutoff shorts, and a crop top that showed off a toned stomach. She also seemed so much paler than Callie remembered. Maybe that was the lighting in the diner?

Then again, she *was* dead. Or was it *un*dead? Callie didn't have a clue, not that it even mattered. All that mattered now was that Maeve had come, just as she said she would, and she was alone. No sign of Elijah or anyone else.

Callie was half lost in thought when Maeve came up to the table and gestured to the bench on the other side. "This seat taken?"

"All yours," Callie said. "Glad you could make it."

"Not like I had anything else to do." Maeve slid into the seat and rested her elbows on the table, watching Callie with her chin in her hands. She had on more makeup than before, including lipstick the color of wine. Or... dried blood. Callie's stomach lurched. Surely that wasn't intentional. And... it *was* lipstick, right? Not——

"Callie, you all right?"

She's just asking to be polite, Callie thought. *She doesn't care how you're doing. Why would she? She doesn't even have a heartbeat.*

"I'm fine," Callie lied. "I'm... well, I was going to say I was sorry for running out on you last night, but I'm not. Not really." It was an uncomfortable truth, but she needed to get it out there. "I just wanted my bracelet. I wanted to go home. I wanted to leave all that weird shit behind."

"I get it," Maeve said. "I would've done the same thing."

Callie blinked. She hadn't expected that response, and she wasn't sure what to say. Thankfully, a waitress in a purple apron approached their table, took out a pen and pad, and offered the women a winning smile.

"Hey there, what can I getcha?"

"Water," Callie said. She slid her laminated menu across the table to Maeve. "And French fries. No ketchup or anything. Thank you."

Maeve studied the menu. "Can I get... the vanilla milkshake? And a side of fries. Thanks."

"Salt doesn't bother you?" Callie asked.

Maeve wrinkled her nose. "Salt's fine. No blood pressure issues. Healthy as a horse." She gave the waitress a disarming smile. "I think that's it for us."

"All right. I'll get that out for ya soon. Holler if you need me. I'm Sharon."

"Thank you, Sharon." Callie waited until the waitress had walked away to lean in closer to Maeve. She lowered her voice so no one would overhear them. "I don't want to talk about the bracelet or the dancing, to be honest. I want to talk about vampires."

"Cut right to it, don't you?" Maeve smirked. "You're not gonna wait for your food?"

Maeve's lipstick was going to kill Callie. She couldn't stop looking at Maeve's mouth. The shade was more blood than wine, but it wasn't all that bad. In fact, it suited Maeve. And Callie wanted to try it. If they were friends, she might have asked Maeve if she could. Right now, she couldn't fathom even asking where she'd gotten it.

"I'm assuming you have a lot to tell me, so no." She was only half joking. "You said Elijah was dangerous, but you're the one who turned into a monster. You... you and Tahlia attacked that cat in the alley."

Maeve's features softened. "I wish you hadn't seen that."

"Me too."

"It wasn't right. T and I try not to get that hungry, but sometimes it's unavoidable." She sighed. "If we fed on humans, we wouldn't get like that, but we don't want to feed on humans."

"Why don't you?"

"I'm not a murderer, Callie. I don't like that side of me."

"But... don't you have to kill to live? Don't you *have* to murder?"

Maeve took a long, measured breath that told Callie almost everything about how wrong she was. How different was Maeve than what she expected? How different were *any* of the vampires?

"I'm like... a vampire vegetarian if you can think of it that way. But I didn't come here to talk about me, or about vampires, although I guess that's inevitable."

The waitress came back with their food and drinks. She set their straws down on the table and smiled before sauntering off again. Callie unwrapped a straw and stabbed it into her water. She grabbed a fry from the plate and popped it into her mouth. The hot potato starch turned to powder in her mouth, tasting like dirt or metal or something else not fit for human consumption. She choked and gagged, covering her mouth. Her eyes widened and her face paled.

"Something the matter?" Maeve asked.

"I..." Callie couldn't get the words to come out. The fry clogged her throat. She cleared it, coughed again, and ran to the bathroom.

Maeve came after her. "Callie."

Callie barely pushed through the swinging door and hunched over the toilet in the first stall before her stomach heaved. Her jaw dropped open and ashes dropped into the toilet, spreading in the bowl and coating the top of the water until they got wet enough to sink. The ashes formed a gray-brown paste as they oozed down the drain.

Callie staggered against the side wall of the stall,

covering her mouth. Her tongue and throat felt the driest they ever have, despite her having vomited. But... she'd thrown up French fries, hadn't she?

"That's what I was afraid of," Maeve said.

Cautiously, with a hand still braced against the plastic of the stall, she crept forward toward the toilet. If she didn't look, she could pretend that everything was normal. Then again, if she didn't look, she'd never know for sure whether she could trust her senses.

Callie did exactly what she knew she had to do. Before she could change her mind, she looked into the toilet.

Ashes coated the bottom of the bowl, not the remnants of a French fry. She coughed into her hand and dust coated her fingers.

"What the hell?" Callie asked.

"You okay?" Maeve asked.

"I don't know. You tell me." Callie leaned against the side of the stall. "What happened, Maeve? What's going on?"

"You threw up... ashes. A mouthful of ashes." Maeve looked away from Callie. "It's a symptom."

"A symptom of what?" Callie asked.

Maeve's face fell. "Did Elijah give you anything last night? Anything to eat or drink?"

"No," Callie said. "Wait, yes. Wine at Indigo."

"You saw him order it?" Maeve asked. "Saw the bartender pour it and everything?"

Callie frowned. She hadn't seen it. "He just brought it to me. I didn't think..."

"Have you felt sick at all today? Before we came here this evening?"

Callie frowned. "I thought it was a hangover."

"And you only had one glass of wine?"

"Yeah," Callie said. Something didn't add up. "Do you

think he roofied me?"

"No. Not exactly." Maeve flipped her hair over her shoulder. "He wouldn't... that's not his style. But I think, I mean, he put *something* in it. Did the drink taste funny?"

"Yeah, tasted metallic. I thought it was the cup."

"Clever bastard. Shit." Maeve went over to the swinging bathroom door and locked it. "Callie, he gave you his blood. You drank Elijah's blood. I'm sorry."

Everything tipped sideways. Callie braced her hands against the table to keep from passing out. Blood? There was no way she'd had blood.

"It didn't taste like blood," said Callie.

"It wouldn't have—ours doesn't. It doesn't taste like human blood. It's... spicy." Maeve's pained expression grew tighter. "It mixes more easily, but Callie... when a human drinks a vampire's blood, it's more than gross. It's dangerous."

Callie's stomach twisted. "Is it going to kill me?"

"Yes. And... no. Not in the way you're thinking. You'll turn, become one of us. A vampire."

"When?" Callie's voice pitched higher. "I mean, how long?"

"Three days," said Maeve.

Callie gawked at her. "Three days? That's it? Three days before I turn into a monster?"

Maeve frowned. "I don't love *monster*."

"Vampire," said Callie. "Whatever."

Maeve was quiet for a moment. She finally returned her gaze to Callie. "Yeah, Callie. Three days."

"And there's nothing I can do to stop it?"

Fuck, she didn't want to be a vampire. She didn't want to die. *She didn't want to be a vampire.*

Someone knocked on the door leading into the

bathroom.

"Out of order," Maeve said. She lowered her voice. "Look, Callie. I'll be honest with you. I think I at least owe you that much. There *is* a way to reverse the turning, or to go back to being human after you've turned. But it's difficult, and for our purposes, I don't think it's worth even considering."

Callie leaned forward again. "So, why won't you tell me?"

"You'd have to kill the vamp who sired you. Turned you, that is." She paused. "You'd need to pierce his skin with a stake and literally turn him to dust."

Great, she'd have to stake Elijah. Callie's heart beat in her ears so loudly she thought Maeve could hear it. A thousand different questions swirled around her head, but she could only put her voice to one of them.

"At least tell me why food tastes like shit," said Callie. "You ordered a milkshake and fries, so I'm guessing you weren't going to just puke those up like me."

"Once you turn, anything but blood tastes awful," Maeve said. "I mean, it does literally turn to ash in your mouth too. It's a spit thing. You're venomous—the venom paralyzes our victims long enough for us to drink from them."

Callie shuddered. "Can we just... should we go out to my car and talk about this there?"

"If that's what you want."

"It is."

"Lead the way."

Maeve stepped back and let Callie pass her. As she passed the mirrors at the sink, Callie thought her reflection wavered, but maybe puking or shock had fucked up her senses. She washed her hands and cast a look at Maeve.

"What about our bill? You intending to pay that?"

"Let me handle it," she said. "I'll meet you outside."

THE SCANT STREETLIGHTS outside the Gemstone Diner did little to keep the darkness at bay. Callie sat on a bench by the front door, staring out at the sea of vehicles. She still couldn't believe what she'd learned in the bathroom. Things just kept getting worse and showed no sign of stopping.

Sure, she supposed she had a way out now. She could kill Elijah. But she'd never even thought about murder before. Vampire or not, that was what it would be.

Callie hugged herself. She had to get in touch with Ramsay. As soon as she could figure out how to tell him about their predicament, she'd apologize and everything.

Maeve came out a minute later. "Squared away. Which car is yours?"

"Did you compel her to give us everything for free?" asked Callie. She wasn't sure why she'd asked when she already knew the answer.

"Yes," Maeve said. "I'm not lying to you. Do you trust me now?"

"No," Callie said. "But I have no choice."

They trekked to Callie's car in silence. Callie slipped into the driver's seat and looked pointedly at Maeve, who stood outside with her hand on the door.

"Need an invitation," said Maeve.

"Jesus. Come in."

Maeve got into the car and closed the door. "I'm just going to talk, if that's okay."

"I'm sure as hell not going to stop you," said Callie.

"About the venom thing and food," Maeve said. "When you're first turned, the levels are off the charts. That's why you can't eat food. After you drink blood, that's not a problem anymore. We don't need food, but milkshakes and fries are delicious, so you know."

Callie raised an eyebrow. "Another myth down, I guess. But does that mean the whole 'puking ash' thing isn't going away soon?"

"Nope," said Maeve. "Not before three days is up. At least, not unless you want to chow down on an animal."

The memory of the cat brought forth a shiver of revulsion, and Callie gulped. She ate meat, but that was different. She'd never actually killed a living thing before.

A tense silence settled between them. Callie stared straight out the windshield, chewing her lip. Maeve looked directly at her.

"I'm sorry for compelling the waitress," Maeve said. "I shouldn't have done that. I'm sorry."

"I don't care about the waitress," Callie answered.

Maeve sighed. "I don't like feeling like people only like me because I push them to. It's too... coercive. And depressing. You can never tell whether someone's really interested. That's why I wouldn't compel..." She let her voice trail off. "You don't have to worry about being compelled around me."

She likes me, Callie thought. *Everything at the club was just her, then. Not an act. Unless it's still an act. But no, that made* little sense. Maeve had nothing to gain anymore.

"I worried you were working with Elijah," Callie said. "I still do, I guess."

"I'm never—well, not *never*. But I don't enjoy working with him." Maeve touched Callie's knee. "Did you think this was a trap?"

"I didn't know what to think," said Callie, and that was the truth. "I also didn't know if there was anybody else."

"You mean other vampires," said Maeve. "Besides our trailer gang."

Callie nodded. For all she knew, Elijah had converted half the town.

"Callie," Maeve said. "Listen. About what I came here to tell you... Ramsay drank your sire's blood. Your brother's turning, too."

For Callie, the world stopped spinning. She felt like passing out. She pushed Maeve's hand away and stared out the side window. How the fuck could this get worse?

"I'm sorry," said Maeve. "I should've said right away, but it didn't feel right in the diner. Not with other people around. Not when I didn't know how you'd react."

Cold sweat beaded on Callie's face. Her eyes stung, but she couldn't cry. "How much time does he have left?" Ramsay had spent a decent chunk of time with Jabari, and he could have had as little as a day left before he transformed. She panicked. "When did Jabari do it?"

"Last night, if he wasn't lying," Maeve said. "Elijah let him have the rest of your drink. I guess Ramsay took it with no questions asked."

"Fucking... of *course*." Callie's fist pounded against the steering wheel. "That means Ramsay has about as much time left as I do."

"Unfortunately, you're right," Maeve said. "It's... not scary turning, although you might be thinking that. I barely remember the time before, let alone between."

"Will it hurt?" Callie asked, though she didn't even care.

"Like hell," Maeve said. "You die and come back, become something else. Something... darker. Deeper and stronger."

Callie paled. "Somehow I didn't think I would die."

"Everyone does sometime."

Callie's throat slammed shut. She thought back to the

beach, the rain, the car. Becca. She put her hand over her bracelet. She chewed the inside of her cheek and tried to think about literally anything but the one thing she could think of. It was often the only thing lately.

What would Becca say if she were there? How would she feel about Callie meeting up with Maeve? About her drinking blood, turning into a vampire?

Callie swallowed hard. "So, unless we kill my sire, there's nothing we can do. We'll both turn no matter what. Is that the gist?"

"Unfortunately." Maeve touched Callie's chin and turned her face toward her. Callie didn't resist.

"You'll need blood," Maeve said. "Sooner rather than later. Sooner, so you can control it."

Although she didn't come out and say it, Callie understood what Maeve was really asking: did she want to become a full-fledged, human-eating vampire, or would she drink from alley cats? How much of a monster was she willing to be?

God, but she was *hungry*.

"Do you think Jabari told Ramsay what's going on?" Callie asked.

"No, I don't think Ramsay has a clue what's going on." Maeve's expression darkened again. "Jabari... has a habit of turning people without their consent."

"I'd say Elijah does too," Callie said, "all things considered."

"You're the first he's done that with. I'm not sure why he did it, either. It's not like him to do something so reckless unless he has some ulterior motive."

Maeve was staring at Callie again. This time, it didn't unnerve her. Maeve's hand drifted back to Callie's face, knuckles brushing her cheek. Callie leaned into the contact.

"Let me do something for you," Maeve said. "You can drink from me. It'll buy you some time. It's not ideal, but it's convenient. Would you be okay with that?"

As if deciding for her, Callie's stomach roared. Color tinged her cheeks. "Would I have to hurt you to do it?"

"No," Maeve said. "I'll set it up for you. All you have to do is drink."

With Callie watching, Maeve lifted an arm to her mouth and scraped her teeth against her wrist. A red line of blood bubbled up from the cut. The sight of it dizzied Callie, evoked the urge to eat Maeve whole.

Maeve's other hand grabbed the back of Callie's neck. She urged her toward the wound. "Go on, Callie. Drink."

Instinct made Callie lunge and slot her mouth over the blood. Saliva spread over Maeve's skin as Callie's jaw clamped down, gums tearing as her fangs came out. The pain was nothing compared to the sheer pleasure of Maeve's blood coating her tongue. Callie sucked on her, *hard*, swallowing as much as she could get.

Maeve's hand tightened in Callie's hair and jerked her head back, away from the blood. Callie hissed.

"*Enough*," Maeve said. "You're done now."

Callie blinked at her. She wasn't sure how long she'd been feeding; just knew she'd blacked out. It was like someone else had done the work for her.

"You should go home now," said Maeve.

Callie's pulse was slow and steady. Blood still sat on her tongue. At the back of her throat. She wanted to say something to Maeve, maybe apologize, but she couldn't find the words. She wasn't sorry.

Maeve opened the door and got out of the car. Callie strapped in and started the engine.

10

It was almost midnight when Callie got home, and the moon cast long shadows of the trees beside the driveway. Callie prayed the sound of the car pulling up hadn't woken her mother. She'd surely catch hell if it had.

When Callie opened the door she jumped, startled to find her mother sitting on the couch in the living room. The house was dark save a lamp on Susan's left. She dropped the book she'd been reading and stood.

"You waited up for me," said Callie.

"I just got in from work," she said. "I didn't expect to beat you."

"Where's Ramsay?" Callie asked.

Her mother's lips formed a tight line. "He isn't with you?"

Callie hesitated. Was she supposed to be his alibi? If so, he had said nothing about it. Besides, the way they'd left things earlier led her to believe he wanted nothing to do with her. Which was going to be a serious problem, what with the whole both-of-them-turning-into-vampires thing.

He didn't even know that was happening yet. Callie doubted Jabari had told him.

"I—no." Callie was too dazed from drinking blood to lie about her brother. "He's... he went out with somebody. Someone he met on a dating app."

"Okay," said Susan. "I get it. We move to a new town. We're all still grieving her, Callie, we all..." She let her voice trail off. Her eyes were wet with tears, but she blinked them away before they fell. Callie felt a tug in her chest. "Well, it can't be easy. Believe me, it's difficult for me too. It's a hell of a lot harder for me to make friends than the two of you, but I can only imagine—"

"That's where I was," Callie said. "Out with friends. I thought you'd be happy to hear that."

Her mom's expression softened. "Oh, sweetheart. I am. Of course I am. It's like I was telling Derek—"

Callie frowned. "Who?"

"The guy from the boardwalk. You met him. Remember?" When Callie shook her head, her mom elaborated. "My boss from the restaurant."

"You confide in him?" asked Callie.

"I'm glad we're talking about Derek now," her mother said. "I wasn't sure how I was going to bring this up to you and Ramsay, but... well, Derek asked me... Derek asked if I wanted to go out on a date with him."

Callie's eyebrows shot into her hairline. Whatever she'd expected her mother to say, it certainly wasn't that. Hell, they'd only been in town for... what, a few weeks? Most of their boxes still sat around unpacked. They even had tape on them still, and they'd only just taken the SOLD sign off the front yard two days ago.

"You've never had an issue with me going out before," her mother said.

"You hardly know Derek. You just met him."

"And you just met your friends. Still, you're expecting me to be okay with that when you're clearly not okay with this?"

Callie's blood boiled. Her stomach burned. She was riding a tsunami of emotions and still hadn't come down from hearing Maeve's news that she and Ramsay were turning. Maybe she was being irrational, but her mom needed to hear it.

"Your men," Callie started. "You have awful taste in men, mom. One right after another, and the new ones always somehow worse than all the old ones put together. Who was that guy, the one who said Becca was—"

"Don't bring that up now." Callie's mom's face had gone stony too. Her jaw clenched. "We've all moved past that. Even Becca said—"

"Maybe we didn't all move past it after all. You should ask Ramsay if he ever 'moved past' you dating the guy who locked him in the bathroom and screamed Bible verses at him for two hours. Or maybe we should talk about the man who peed in bottles and left them all around our house for me to trip over. What about him?" Callie scowled at her mother. Her hands had clenched into fists while she was talking and her fingernails bit into her palms. Still, she didn't relax. She couldn't. It was time for it all to come out.

"The guy who slapped my ass," she said. "The one who left cigarette burns on the couch. The one who let our cat out, the one who—"

"Calliope, stop." Her mother's voice was soft, but firm. Tighter than Callie had heard it in years. "You have no right to question my choices when you won't even tell me who you've been out with or where you're going or how long you're going to be there. You and Ramsay both think you can just... do whatever the hell you want to now, like nothing even matters."

Callie's chest rose and fell as she tried to get her breathing under control. The rage was an electric whip against her spine.

"You'd never talk like this to Becca."

"Yeah, well maybe I should have."

"Maybe you should have done a lot of things."

"I'm going out with Derek, Callie. I'm a grown woman, *and* I'm your mother. I don't have to answer to you. It's only one date. End of discussion."

"Okay." Callie's grip on her keys tightened. She stepped back over the threshold with one hand on the handle of the door. "If that's how it's going to be."

"What's that supposed to mean?"

Callie slammed the door instead of giving her an answer. She yanked open her car door, clambered back in, and started the engine—all while sneaking glances at the front door. It was only when her mother didn't come after her that Callie realized she'd wanted her to.

11

The Starlight Boardwalk was deserted. Callie texted Maeve. She sat shivering in the parking lot with the windows down, hoping the sea breeze would blow away her tension.

Shit, she'd never had a fight like that with her mother. Even in the accident's wake, when it was tense between them and everyone was angry at everyone for everything—for Becca being gone, for her hair on the bathroom floor, for the off-black shade of Ramsay's funeral suit—they'd never gotten so personal. Even as a teenager, Callie hadn't fought much with her mother.

Maybe Callie was becoming a monster after all.

Callie swallowed the lump in her throat. She kept checking her phone, but Maeve hadn't texted her back. Nothing from Ramsay either. Or Elijah, but that didn't surprise her. Hell, she'd be lying if she said that wasn't a relief.

Small favors and all that.

A shadow at the corner of her eye seized her attention.

Maeve rapped her knuckles against the passenger window. Callie still jumped.

"Jesus Christ." She rolled the window down so Maeve could lean on the door and talk to her. "You scared the hell out of me."

"If only, right?" Maeve winked. Callie groaned.

"You gonna let me in or what?" Maeve said. "It's getting cold out here."

"Vampires get cold?"

"This one does. Come on, Callie." Maeve pouted at her.

"Fuck. Okay, hold on." Callie disengaged the manual locks. Maeve reached through the open window and popped the door open. She got in and slammed it shut so hard that if the window had been up, she probably would've broken it.

"Maeve! Holy shit."

Maeve winced. "I'm sorry. I forget my strength, et cetera."

Callie took a minute to look her over. She'd changed into something different since the diner, a black bodycon dress that clung to her body like it was nothing. Silver bracelets jangled on her wrists, matching her septum ring and the small hoops running up and down her ears. Lipstick—or dried blood—colored her mouth. Didn't matter which it was. Callie wanted to taste it.

She felt a pang of fear unlike she'd felt around anyone besides Elijah and certainly not with Maeve. Was she being compelled again? Maybe Maeve had lied to her before. Maybe she'd—

"Callie." Maeve snapped her fingers. Callie blushed. "Where'd you go?"

She wasn't sure it was safe to say. Then again, she'd already invited Maeve to sit in the car with her. Callie hesitated, racking her brain for something intelligent to say. Instead, she reached across Maeve's lap and rolled the window up.

Maeve's hand caught her wrist before she could pull away. When Callie met her eyes, she relaxed her grip a little. Callie didn't pull her arm back. They sat there staring at each other. Callie wasn't even sure she was still breathing.

"I told you, I won't lie to you. If you can't trust me, it'll kill me."

Maeve's admission surprised her. "What do you mean?"

"Shit. This isn't what I wanted to say. When we were at the diner, that was when I should have said... Christ, I should stop now. Ask you to kick me out of your car and drive off without me. Go home to your mom. Take care of your brother."

"Don't," Callie said. She wanted to say so much more but feared her words might break the fragile thing that stretched between them. "Maeve, please. I need—"

"You need to listen," Maeve hissed, but her eyes were still soft. Anyone besides Callie might still have been afraid —after all, she was a monster.

Not to me, thought Callie. Never.

"I'm listening," she said.

"Elijah got you all wrapped up in this and it really fucking sucks. I wish we'd met without his interference. I wish I hadn't agreed to help him at the club, to keep that bracelet from you." Maeve's voice caught, and she cleared her throat.

"You're the only person in decades to make me feel anything but hollow and as much as that scares me, what scares me more is never letting you know and losing you to someone shitty. Maybe... to Elijah."

"Maeve, not Elijah."

"You should hate me. I would hate me. You have every right to. And, once this is all resolved, once you and Ramsay get back to normal..." She swallowed. "I just... fuck me, I don't know how to even say this."

"Just say it."

"I like you. I really like you." She squeezed Callie's wrist. "And I'm scared you don't give half a shit about me, but I'd understand it and that's the worst part. For so long, I've only been with Elijah and Tahlia and some one-offs here and there but... I've wanted to kiss you since the bar, Callie. Wanted to push you against the wall and put my hand up your skirt. Wanted—"

Callie surged forward and caught Maeve's mouth with hers. Their lips slanted over each other; Maeve's tongue darted out to touch the tip of Callie's. Eager, but not presumptuous. Callie deepened the kiss and Maeve jerked her arm, pulling her closer.

"Is this okay?" Callie asked.

"God, yes," said Maeve. "Come over here."

Shakily, Callie climbed over the console and onto Maeve's lap. Her thighs bracketed Maeve's slim hips. They kissed again, and for a long time, the kissing was enough until it wasn't anymore, it wasn't even close, and Maeve's hand closed on Callie's breast as Callie ground against her.

Fuck. It felt so good. She hadn't felt good in a long time. And never like this.

In high school, Callie had fooled around with some women. Mostly straight friends at sleepovers whose parents' liquor made them bold, a few less straight classmates at parties here and there. She'd slept with maybe two women in her life. Before Neap Bay, she'd only ever fallen hard for men—or for the masculine-presenting.

With Maeve, it was different. Maeve set her on fire.

When they broke apart to catch their breath, they both were grinning. Callie smiled so hard her face ached.

"Can't fucking believe it," Maeve said. "Can't fucking believe I didn't kiss you sooner. Cal, you taste *so* fucking good."

"Want to taste you too." Callie pressed her mouth to the side of Maeve's neck. To her collarbone. "All over."

Maeve let out a shaky breath. "I just can't fucking believe this. I've never—I mean, not *never*—"

"Less talking," said Callie. "Show me instead."

Maeve slid her hand up Callie's shirt and under the cup of her bra. Callie's breath hitched. Jesus, how long had it been since someone had touched her like this?

They kissed again, hungry and open-mouthed, and Callie kept forgetting to breathe. The insatiable need to feed gnawed at her too, made so much worse by Maeve's proximity. If Maeve had had a pulse, Callie wasn't sure she would have been able to resist.

She pulled back, looking Maeve in the eyes. "Maeve, I need... God, I need blood. It's bad. I don't think—."

"Let me help you drown the thoughts out," she said. "Just focus on me."

Callie nodded. Maeve kneaded her breast, thumb moving over her nipple. Callie sucked in another breath. She wanted to make Maeve feel good too, wanted to touch her all over. Wanted to feel her skin against hers and find out how well their bodies fit together. If it was anything like what she'd glimpsed in the club, she was more than ready for it.

A thought flashed across Callie's mind: *how many times had Maeve done this? How many people—*

"I swear to God, I can feel you thinking," Maeve said. "Thought I told you to focus on me."

Callie swallowed and did what she was told. The confines of the car gave them limited room to move, but Maeve held Callie's hip with one hand and let the fingertips of her other graze just inside Callie's waistband. Callie tilted her hips toward Maeve, scooting as close to her as the car would allow. Maeve met her gaze, holding it for a moment, before her eyes darkened and her hand slid into Callie's panties, fingers brushing her center.

"Jesus," Callie hissed.

"Still good?" Maeve murmured.

Callie could only nod. Maeve was quickly making her incapable of speech, and she doubted that was going to get any better with time and the downward trajectory of Maeve's hand.

"Want to taste you," Maeve said. The admission made Callie's stomach flutter and heat pool between her legs. "Wish we weren't in a fucking car."

"Next time," Callie said.

"Yeah? I'll hold you to it."

Maeve's fingers curled up into her without warning. She captured Callie's mouth with hers again, working Callie as Callie's hips bucked into Maeve's palm.

"Maeve." Callie wanted to moan, but all she could manage was Maeve's name. Delicious tension coiled like a serpent in her core. Maeve kept moving inside her, keeping a steady pace, thumb lazily stroking Callie. "Maeve, you need to slow down, I'm going to—"

"Come?" Maeve asked. Callie swore she heard the smirk behind her voice. "What do you think I want you to do?"

Christ, Callie thought. *She's going to kill me.* And maybe she was, but honestly? What a way to go.

"So sweet," Maeve murmured. "Never thought you'd be this sweet."

Even though she already had Maeve's fingers inside her —and that what Maeve was saying was tame, all things considered—Callie blushed.

When Callie came, she clamped down on Maeve's fingers and trembled against her as the universe exploded into pinpoints of light and dazzling sensations under her skin.

"Maeve," she murmured. "Maeve... I want to make you feel good, too."

Maeve dragged her fingers out of Callie and slipped them into her mouth. She offered Callie no response, only closed her lips and sucked.

Callie drew in a sharp breath. Shit. "Want to make you feel good *now*."

Somehow, she clambered over the center console and toward the back seat, dragging Maeve along with her.

"So much for sweet," Maeve said between kisses.

"I'll be whatever you want me to be," Callie panted.

They made out there for a while, Callie's body pinned beneath Maeve's. Callie got a wicked glint in her eyes and flipped them, closing her teeth on Maeve's neck. This close, Maeve smelled like steel. Cold and antiseptic. It made little sense.

Callie pulled back, frowning down at Maeve. "Why do you smell like...?"

"Metal?" Maeve finished. "Yeah, that's the vampire in you realizing I'm not a good food source. It's getting stronger." Her forehead wrinkled. Callie kissed her neck and made her way down to Maeve's breasts. Maeve sighed.

"I want to bite you, but not like that," said Callie. "I want to know what you taste like, though. Think there's plenty of room back here for that."

"You want to go down on me?" Maeve asked.

"God, yes. I would love to."

"Let me just... hike up my skirt..."

Callie watched as Maeve dragged the tight fabric up her hips, revealing toned white thighs that all but glinted in the moonlight. *Jesus Christ, this woman is exquisite*, Callie thought.

"Penny for your thoughts," Maeve said.

Callie kissed her. It was slow, but insistent. When she pulled away, she expected to see Maeve flushed, but she wasn't. Then, she realized: *Vampire. No heartbeat, no blood flow.* But no blood flow meant no orgasm, right?

"Maeve," Callie said. "Can I make you come?"

"You tell me." Maeve winked.

"You know what I mean. Your blood... it's like, stagnant or something, isn't it?" Callie asked. "So... it can't... increase anywhere, right?"

"I can come," Maeve said. "Don't worry about it."

Callie was suddenly nervous, like she'd never done this before. Truth was, she'd only been with a couple of women, and none as intimidating as Maeve. What if she wasn't any good at this?

"Hey." Maeve touched her face, thumb skimming over Callie's jaw line. "It's okay. You don't have to do anything you don't want to."

Callie flushed again. "I definitely want to. Wanting's not the problem."

"You can't mess it up. I promise."

Callie exhaled. She knew Maeve was right, and she knew she wanted to make Maeve feel good. She wanted to make her come. And she would do whatever it took to help get her there.

She gripped Maeve's hips and scooted down to rest between her legs. She could feel how cold Maeve was, and it was jarring. If she hadn't known Maeve was a vampire, it would have freaked her out.

Callie reached up and tugged Maeve's underwear off. She tossed it to the floor. Black lace. Flimsy. Had Maeve expected this?

Callie slid her hands up Maeve's legs and parted her thighs. A cell phone chime interrupted her.

Maeve and Callie looked at each other. The phone chimed again, then started buzzing on the console. It was too loud to ignore.

"Of course," Maeve said.

"Just... give me a second." Callie straightened up as best she could and picked up the phone. She clicked the button on the side to stop it from ringing. Three texts and a missed call, all from her mother. Fantastic. Still, since the phone had interrupted their session, it was worth checking the texts.

Know you're mad at me. Just be safe

And:

Ramsay still hasn't come home. Is he with you?

And even:

Please look for Ramsay. Please bring him home. I don't care if you're both angry with me.

Please keep each other safe.

She had said nothing about their argument beyond acknowledging Callie's anger, and Callie felt a stab of guilt over how she'd reacted. She couldn't help thinking about Becca, how their mother hadn't gotten the chance to say goodbye. How if something happened to Callie, too, she'd be in the same situation.

"Honey," Maeve said. "What's wrong?"

No one had ever called her *honey* in her life. Coming from Maeve, she liked it.

"I just... it's my mom. She wants me to find Ramsay." Callie brushed off another pang of guilt. She hadn't been thinking about her brother. "We had a fight, and I ran out on her, but I thought Ramsay would be back before me. I don't know where he is."

Maeve studied Callie for a moment. "We can check Jabari's trailer. They might still be around here."

She stretched to retrieve her underwear and slid them back on. Maeve readjusted her skirt and pressed a hand against her hair.

"Do I look like I've had sex?"

Callie shook her head. "You look unfulfilled. I'm sorry."

"Plenty of time for that later, okay? I'm a big girl." She winked again. "I'll be fine, honey. Promise. I still had fun."

"Yeah?"

"Yeah. Let's find your brother."

Maeve leaned over and kissed her. When they broke apart, Callie readjusted her clothes and went to fix her hair in the mirror—but, of course, there was nothing there. She did a double take. Neither of them had reflections.

"Fuck," said Callie. "Now, I don't show up in mirrors."

"You're getting close," Maeve said. "I'm sorry."

It was just another part of Callie's shitty situation. The

sooner she found Ramsay, the better off they'd be. Maybe then she would have time to mourn the loss of looking in mirrors.

"Ready?" asked Callie.

Maeve nodded. "Let's go."

12

Callie felt guilty about spending so much time with Maeve. By the time they trekked over to Jabari's trailer, neither he nor her brother was anywhere to be found. She was glad that Maeve had come with her to lift her battered spirits.

"Probably headed home," Maeve reassured her. "Jabari... I dunno, walked him home or something. Does that sound reasonable?"

"It's a long way to walk. He would've called me," Callie said. As she said it, she questioned its certainty. The last time they spoke, he'd been angry with her. Maybe he was trying to steer clear of her as much as possible.

"We could check with Elijah," Maeve said.

Callie winced. She wasn't sure she could be around him again, not unless she could kill him. She still had no clue how to make that one happen.

"I know he's the last person you want to see," said Maeve. "But he might help us. He might tell us where your brother is, at least."

She was right. They had no other leads. Callie groaned and relented.

They walked over to Elijah's trailer and Callie's heart rose in her throat. The last time she'd been around Elijah, he'd turned her. She couldn't trust a word he said. He might have been their only option, but that didn't mean she liked it.

"You can wait out here," Maeve offered.

"I want to find my brother, Maeve. I don't care what it takes."

When Maeve tried the handle of the door, it was unlocked. She pushed and gestured for Callie to enter. The first thing she saw was Ramsay.

Callie was more angry than surprised. He lay on the bed in a heap of limbs and bare skin with Jabari and Elijah, both of whom weren't the least bit bothered by Callie and Maeve's intrusion. As the light from the open door fell in on them, they blinked but didn't break apart.

"Ramsay," Callie said.

"Yeah." His voice was rough with sleep, though it didn't look like too much sleeping had been going on in there. "What are you doing? Why didn't you knock?"

"What the fuck?" Callie asked. "Why didn't I *knock*? Ramsay, you've been missing. Mom's freaking out. Last time I talked to you, you hung up on me. And now, you're here with *Elijah* having a goddamn orgy."

Ramsay's brow furrowed. Shit, she'd forgotten he had no clue what Elijah had done to her—or what Jabari had done to Ramsay. It was probably a bad idea to clue the vampires in to her knowledge of their plans, but she didn't give a fuck anymore.

"Jabari... sired you. Elijah did the same to me." Callie studied his face, waiting for some clue that he understood what she was saying, but Ramsay's face stayed blank. "God damn it, they're vampires. Like... Dracula and shit. They're trying to turn us into vampires too."

Ramsay scoffed. His eyebrows lifted, and he looked at Callie like he didn't know her anymore. "Are you high or something? Jesus."

Jabari looked at Elijah. Elijah's mouth stretched open, fangs glinting in the moonlight. His pupils narrowed into slits and reflected light back at them. *A monster.*

Ramsay's mouth dropped open. He looked like he wanted to scream, but no sound came out. His fists went up like he wanted to deck Elijah, but Jabari grabbed his hands and held them. Ramsay stayed still.

"It's true," Elijah said. "And don't scream. There's no point in it."

"Vampires," Ramsay repeated. "Like... bloodsucking, soul-eating vampires?"

"We don't eat souls," Jabari grumbled.

"And... you *sired* me?" Ramsay asked Jabari. "Whatever the fuck that means."

Jabari groaned. "I fed you some blood. You'll turn soon enough, and none of this shit will make a difference. Elijah got Callie, too."

Ramsay's gaze snapped back to Callie. "It's not just a hangover, is it?"

She shook her head. "According to Maeve, we'll be vamps in three days."

"*Fuck!*" Ramsay shoved Jabari off him and elbowed Elijah out of the way. He slid off the bed and started pulling on the clothing discarded on the floor. Callie averted her eyes as he dressed. "I can't believe this shit. Just when I thought—"

"We should go," Callie said.

"Yeah, you fucking *think*?" Ramsay's face was as red as his hair. "I'm never coming back here, Jesus fucking Christ."

He was so upset, it didn't seem to matter that Elijah sat there looking scary. Slowly, his features morphed back to normal, lips curling into a smirk. Rage simmered beneath the surface of Callie's skin. She swore Maeve could feel it because she reached for Callie's hand and laced their fingers together.

Ramsay paused halfway into his shirt to stare at the contact. "What, and you're just hooking up with them?"

Callie was so outraged, she laughed. "What the fuck are you doing, huh? You're one to fucking talk."

Maeve squeezed Callie's hand, but there was nothing she could say. There was nothing anyone could say to make the situation better.

"Ram," Jabari started. "I didn't mean to—"

"Run along now," said Elijah. "Go, before I change my mind."

Ramsay had his shirt on inside-out. The tag stuck out the back. Callie didn't think it was the right moment to tell him to adjust it. He zipped up his pants and ran a hand through his hair. There was no fixing it. "Let's get the fuck out."

Callie reluctantly dropped Maeve's hand. They exchanged a long look before Callie refocused her attention on Elijah. He was staring. The heat of his gaze raised the hairs on the back of her neck.

"Drive safe," he said.

Callie couldn't shake the feeling that somehow, they were playing right into his hands. Still, she didn't have to dwell on the thought for too long. By the time they got back to the car, the nervous energy Ramsay radiated finally exploded.

"Can't believe my fucking luck," he said. "I meet someone new, and he turns out to be a monster. What are the odds?"

"Gotta be astronomical," Callie replied. "But hey, both of us now."

Ramsay got into the passenger seat, put on his seatbelt, and shut the door. He waited for Callie to get into the car and buckle up before he continued. "So, you and Maeve. Didn't she have your bracelet?"

"It's in the past." Callie turned the car on and checked her rearview mirror. She backed the car out of its space. "Turns out a lot can change in two days."

"You're telling me." Ramsay dragged a hand down his face. She recognized the movement out of the corner of her eye. "You fuck her or what?"

"Jesus!"

"What? I'm asking!"

"You don't have to be so crass," she said.

"Since when are you a prude?"

Callie groaned. She didn't want to have any of this conversation. She knew exactly what he was doing—he was hoping to use her personal drama to deflect from the gravity of their current situation. Maybe he was also still in shock from Maeve's admission.

"This is all so fucking wild," Callie said. "I feel like it's the weirdest dream I've ever had, like I'll wake up at any minute."

Ramsay exhaled through his nose. "Is Elijah dangerous? Is that a part of it?"

"I... I'm not sure. I mean, I guess the entire group's dangerous. They're all vampires." A dead moth stuck to windshield. She pulled the knob to clean it and watched the wipers move as she spoke.

"But... well, Maeve wants to help us. Tahlia, too, I think. Honestly, I'm not really sure where she stands."

"You don't think Maeve acted that way just to get into your pants?" Ramsay asked.

A muscle jerked in Callie's jaw. She didn't want to believe that. Hell, she *didn't* believe that. She hadn't doubted Maeve since they'd met up at the diner. Deep down, somehow, she was certain they could trust her—even if they couldn't trust anybody else.

"No," Callie said. "It's not like that with her."

The streets of Neap Bay were empty at night. It was one a.m. Even the Starlight Boardwalk had closed. No wonder Callie's mother had worried about them.

She felt another stab of guilt. Maybe she'd overreacted. Their mother deserved to be happy, even if it felt like an inconvenience. Even if Callie didn't want to let someone else into their lives.

Besides, it was one date. It wasn't like her mom was asking Derek to move in with them.

Callie hoped he was a nice guy. Her mother deserved someone nice.

The turn signal blinked as Callie pulled into their neighborhood. Ramsay had said nothing else, and she almost thought he wouldn't, but then:

"Mom's going out with that guy, isn't she?"

Callie almost gaped at him. "How the hell did you know that?"

"I can read you even if you're not my twin," he said. "You always act out when Mom sees someone new."

"Well," Callie countered, "at least I wasn't having a threesome with some monsters."

"Nope," he answered. "Just a twosome."

Callie sighed. Clearly, he didn't want to rehash the

encounter. He was deflecting, but fine, she'd give in. "Mom... she said Derek asked her out. I didn't stick around for the details."

She felt—rather than saw—him raise an eyebrow at her. "Did you storm out of the house?"

Callie winced. "Kind of. But not before I went off on her for a while."

"Shit. What did you say?"

She didn't want to get into it, but she had little choice. "I told her she had shitty taste in men," said Callie. "I... rehashed her whole dating history. She said I had no room to talk because you and I have been staying out late and sneaking around with people she doesn't know."

Ramsay was quiet again. When he spoke, his voice was soft. "Guess we all just... worry like hell about each other."

"More or less," said Callie.

The car turned into their driveway. Callie pulled up to the closed garage door and put the car in park. She let the engine idle.

Too much to go over, she thought.

"What are we going to do?" Ramsay asked.

"I don't know," Callie said. "I need to talk to Maeve about it."

"Fuck, I can't even eat. I tried, and everything just—"

"Turned into ashes," Callie finished. "I'm aware."

She twisted in her seat to face Ramsay. He mirrored her. The glow of her headlights washed his skin out and made him look even paler. Then again, maybe he was just turning. Maybe he'd be completely chalk-colored soon.

Ramsay chewed the inside of his cheek. He shook his head.

"What?" Callie asked.

"I still can't believe it. If Becca were here, she'd think all this was hilarious."

"Becca would never have let us get into this situation in the first place," Callie said. "She sure as shit wouldn't be dumb enough to get turned."

They sat in the idling car for a few minutes. Callie had so much she wanted to say to her brother, but none of it really mattered. The only thing she knew for certain was that they both had to be careful.

"Before we go in," Callie said. "You can't say anything to Mom. Not about the argument, the vampires, getting turned —none of it, okay? She'd never understand."

Ramsay only nodded. After another minute of silence, Callie turned off the car.

13

The words on Callie's laptop screen were blurring together. On the floor, Ramsay didn't seem to do any better. Both had slept late into the next afternoon, but Callie still felt like shit. Judging by Ramsay's groans, his body wasn't running on all cylinders either. His forearm rested over his eyes as though trying to shut out the light, even though Callie had kept the shades drawn.

Sunlight made a burning itch explode across her skin. It was getting worse. They had little time left before they turned into full-fledged vampires.

Or half, Callie thought, *like Maeve and Tahlia. Could I subsist on cat blood for the rest of my life?* She didn't want to think about Maeve feeding her again. It was far too tempting.

Then again, if she became a vampire, who even knew how long the rest of her life could be? Callie assumed they were immortal and couldn't die of sickness or old age or natural causes. They had to be staked or whatever.

God, she didn't want to think about any of that.

"What's it saying?" Ramsay asked.

Callie looked back at the screen. To uncover more information about the transformation, she'd typed "vampirism" into Google. Naturally, that led to Wikipedia, one thing turned into another, and before she knew it, so was so far down the virtual rabbit hole that she'd started reading about spontaneous human combustion and haunted houses and paranormal vloggers.

"Nothing helpful," Callie answered.

So far, all she'd found was a long list of vampire lore from countries all over the world, examples of vampires in popular culture, and explanations and debunkings of "so-called" modern vampires. A vlogger named Terrified in Tokyo touched on the concept of vampires in Japan, but that was it. There was absolutely nothing to suggest what she and Ramsay were going through was anything but an isolated incident.

If they hadn't already met them, Callie might still have believed that vampires didn't exist. Once you'd seen those teeth, though, they weren't easy to forget.

She ran her tongue over her own teeth. Sharp as hell.

"What are we supposed to do if Mom asks why we don't want to go outside?" Ramsay asked.

"We *can* go out," Callie answered. "It just needs to be at night. Besides, I doubt she'll notice. It's so hot, no one is out unless they have somewhere to be."

"Are you implying that we have no social life?"

"I'm not implying. I'm outright saying."

"Ouch, Cal."

"What?" she asked. "Our only actual contacts in Neap Bay besides Mom are a gang of vampire thieves we know nothing about. Besides, our social life should be the last of our concerns."

Ramsay sat up. "Don't say that about our social life."

Callie rolled her eyes. "I can't with you right now."

Ramsay lay back down. "What have you been searching for, anyway? Maybe you need to enter better search terms or whatever."

"Just... vampires," Callie admitted. "Pretty basic stuff."

"Come on. What about 'vampires Neap Bay,' 'Neap Bay legends,' shit like they'd Google in a horror movie?"

"This isn't *Sinister* or *The Ring*."

"Just try it, okay? Jesus."

Callie bit her lip and returned her attention to her laptop. Something about Neap Bay could be a good start. She thought back to their first day at the boardwalk and the missing posters. Her fingers crawled over the keyboard.

Neap Bay disappearances. And there it was, the first result: "Neap Bay's Missing People Problem."

NEAP BAY, CA.— People in this sleepy seaside town are going missing, and experts have no leads. Since the eighties, a rash of unexplained disappearances has many questioning if they're all connected. It is this reporter's opinion that there is more than meets the eye with all these cases.

Take Madison Cowell. When the twenty-two-year-old boardwalk games attendant disappeared in '88, local law enforcement assumed she had run away.

"She made friends with some people she met at the boardwalk," remarked Madison's mother, Victoria Cowell. "I'm worried she's fallen in with the wrong crowd."

"I want Starlight Boardwalk—as well as the Neap Bay Police Department—to take her disappearance seriously," Madison's father, Bryce Cowell said. "I always run background checks on my workers, and I'd expect any other business to do the same. Don't they want to know who's working for them?"

There has been no evidence linking any Starlight Boardwalk employees to Cowell's disappearance. However, when another games attendant went missing six months later, many suspicions were aroused.

When asked about the missing people, Neap Bay Police Chief Roger Deneuve originally had no comment. It wasn't until Deneuve's daughter went missing that the department agreed to say something.

"We're doing everything we can to track down these kids," Chief Deneuve said. "We're asking anyone who might have a lead to come down to the station and talk with us."

Since providing his initial statement, Chief Deneuve and the department have opened an anonymous tip line. "If anyone is uncomfortable speaking to the police in person, they're more than welcome to call in," said the chief.

At the time of writing this article, twelve young people have been confirmed as missing since 1988—Madison Cowell, Peter Rodriguez, Kayla Deneuve, Lacey Shaw, Melissa Navarro, Duncan McKnight, Cynthia Chavez, Jennifer Rojas, Michelle Calhoun, and Reuben Shaffer, Gino Hahn, and Esther Schulman. I suspect yet more instances of missing people to be reported. Representatives of the Starlight Boardwalk have declined to comment on the matter, and police have detained no suspects. Still, how many more people have to disappear before law enforcement does something?

Callie looked up from the laptop. So, the Neap Bay disappearances had been happening for a while—since the late eighties, at least. Tahlia and Maeve said they'd turned in the eighties. That had to be more than a coincidence.

"Find something?" Ramsay asked.

"I need to call Maeve," said Callie. "I think... well, I might have found a lead. She's the only one I trust to help." She twisted in her seat to look at Ramsay again. His eyes were closed, and he looked even paler than he had a few minutes before. If she looked closely, she felt like she could see the veins that pulsed beneath his skin. She could almost smell—

"Fuck." Callie shook her head to clear it. She pinched the bridge of her nose. "If these symptoms don't let up..."

"I know what you mean," he said. "Call Maeve and ask her if there's anything we can do. If you're going to call her anyway about what you found, you might as well get as much out of her as possible."

The implication behind his words made Callie blush. She averted her gaze. "Many people have gone missing. I'm not sure, but a lot of it seems to line up with the boardwalk. With the vampires."

"Jesus," said Ramsay. "Just call her already."

Callie found Maeve's contact information and pressed the phone icon. Maeve picked up on the second ring. Her voice was rough with sleep.

"Hey, honey. Need something?" Callie's stomach fluttered. Shit, she needed to focus.

"Is Elijah... well, there are people going missing," Callie said. "People have *gone* missing. At least twelve since the eighties, when my mom still lived here."

"Whatever you're thinking," Maeve said, "just say it."

"Did you kidnap Madison Cowell?" asked Callie.

"Madison," Maeve repeated. There was silence on the

other end of the line, coupled with crinkling paper, like something was being unwrapped.

"Are you eating something?" Callie asked.

"Leftovers, and please, don't ask me to elaborate on that." Maeve's tone was gentle, but firm. "I don't remember a Madison. Who else is missing?"

Callie returned her attention to the article she'd found. "Uh... like, twelve different people. Give me a second... yeah, here. Peter Rodriguez, Lacey Shaw... Kayla Deneuve, Esther Schulman. Looks like they're all around—"

"Hang on," Maeve said. "I know them. They were victims."

Anger flared at the back of Callie's mind. "You killed them and couldn't remember their names?"

"Not me, honey," said Maeve. "I didn't kill anyone."

Callie didn't want to get into this with her. Not now, when everything between them was going so well, anyway. The less she thought about Maeve as a monster, the better.

"Your friends are killing them," Callie said.

"Yes. It's been us—well, them," Maeve stammered. "I haven't... I mean, I won't lie to you, I was a little bit involved. I didn't drink from anyone, but some of them... I think I helped Elijah lure some of them into our trailers. I wish I hadn't now, but there's no way to go back and change what I did." She let out a long sigh. "I'm a different person now. I feel different."

"Because of me?" Callie asked.

"Not just you. Just... a lot of things," Maeve continued. "I'm sick of Elijah's bullshit excuses."

On the floor, Ramsay groaned. It could have been the lighting, but his skin looked gray. Ashen. He still had his arm thrown over his face so Callie couldn't see his eyes. He still had said nothing while she was talking to Maeve, which was unusual. Usually, Ramsay loved to butt in on her phone calls. He and Becca used to yell things like, "Put your pants back on!" while Callie was talking to someone. She hadn't expected to miss that, but she did.

Ramsay was getting worse. He was turning much faster than Callie. And the worst part of it was that she had no clue what to do.

"Elijah needs to be stopped," Callie said. "And Ramsay... well, I think he's getting worse. Do you think you could come over? I don't know what to do."

Callie felt Maeve's eyebrows raise. "What about your mother?"

"She's out with some guy she met at work. She probably won't be home until later." Callie flushed, suddenly feeling like a teenager plotting a romantic rendezvous. This was mostly for Ramsay's benefit, sure, but she couldn't deny the fact that she looked forward to seeing Maeve again, even in such bizarre circumstances.

"I'll text you my address."

"I don't have a car," Maeve said.

"Shit, that's right." Callie felt like such a moron for forgetting something like that.

"Hell, I'll come and get you. Give me fifteen minutes."

"Will do. And... be careful." Maeve paused. "Honey."

Callie's grin nearly split her face in half. "I'll see you soon. Meet me in the parking lot, okay?"

Ramsay finally moved his arm. His eyes were bloodshot, glassy. For the first time, Callie noticed his lips were also cracked. When he spoke, his voice broke.

"I think I'm gonna die, Cal. I don't wanna die."

Her pulse roared in her ears. Neither had Becca. She thought back to Maeve giving Callie her blood. Could Callie do the same thing for Ramsay?

Selfishly, she couldn't. She was worried he might kill her.

"Maeve's coming over. I'm sure she can help. Just hang on, all right?" said Callie. "Everything will be okay."

She only wished she could believe it.

14

W hen Callie pulled up to the Starlight Boardwalk, Maeve leaned against a pole, holding an umbrella to keep the sun at bay. *Smart*, Callie thought.

Although it was late afternoon, there was still enough sun to hurt. On the way to the boardwalk, Callie's thighs and arms itched where the sun hit them. Now she was shaded, but her skin still tingled. She wasn't even a full-fledged vampire, so she couldn't imagine what the others went through.

She made a mental note to ask Maeve more about her own condition and what would happen to Callie and Ramsay if they chose to never feed. She assumed they'd die, but maybe there was more to it than that. She'd have to ask Maeve.

Maeve got into the car and leaned over the center console to pull Callie into a kiss. It was quick, and Callie wanted more, but there wasn't time for that.

"Tell me what's going on," Maeve said.

Callie pulled out of the lot and headed back to her

house. Along the way, she told Maeve how shitty she and Ramsay had been feeling, how she'd seen him deteriorating at a faster rate than she was. She told Maeve she was terrified. She didn't want to die, but she didn't want to lose her brother.

By the time they pulled into Callie's driveway, Callie felt like she'd gone through the emotional wringer. While they drove, Maeve's hand had settled on her bare thigh. As the car idled, her hand lingered. Her fingers were cold but comforting. Callie covered Maeve's hand with her own.

"I don't know what to do, and I have no one else to turn to. If we can't get Ramsay help..."

"Don't worry about that yet," Maeve said. "I'm here to help however I can."

They got out of the car and went into the house. At first, Callie thought Ramsay had left. The silence inside was deafening.

"Ramsay," Callie called. A groan came from upstairs. That meant he hadn't moved. He was still lying on her floor.

Callie sighed. "Come down here."

Ramsay groaned again, but Callie could hear him moving around up there. Maeve looked at her, biting her bottom lip. Callie only shrugged.

"He... doesn't look right," Callie said. "Should I be afraid of him?"

"No," Maeve said, a little too quickly. "Well, maybe not. It depends. If he's turned already, his bloodlust might drive him to hurt you. If he tries anything, I'll put him on his ass."

Ramsay rounded the corner at the top of the stairs and descended. He lifted a hand and pointed to something behind Callie. "What's that?"

Callie looked back over her shoulder at the kitchen. A bottle of red wine sat unopened on the counter. She hadn't noticed it before. It had a gold ribbon tied around it, twisted up into a bow. Had her mother done that? Maybe it was a peace offering. At any rate, she figured she, Ramsay, and Maeve could all use a little alcohol.

She grabbed the bottle of wine and a corkscrew, eyeing Ramsay warily.

"How do you feel?" she asked.

"Like I'm dying," he said. He looked at Maeve. "That's what's happening to me, isn't it?"

"Yeah," Maeve said. "You look like shit."

"Thanks a lot, asshole." But the ghost of a smile played on his lips. "Pour me a glass of that, Callie."

"I'd like some too," said Maeve.

Callie stuck the sharp point of the corkscrew into the cork of the bottle and twisted. It came out with a satisfying pop. Before she could grab some glasses, Ramsay snatched the bottle from her hands. He tipped it into his mouth and drank it.

"Christ," Callie said.

Ramsay wiped his mouth with the back of his hand. "I'm *dying*. I should get to drink it all."

"So am I," Callie argued.

"Not quite," Maeve said. "Ramsay is... well, he's turning much faster than you. He hasn't drunk from anybody." She looked at the bottle in Ramsay's hands. "Once he turns, we can't do shit unless we kill his sire."

"On top of all this, the wine tastes bad," said Ramsay.

"It tastes like shit because it's old," said Callie. "Label says the 1910s."

"Why would anyone want that?" he asked.

"People like old things." Callie reached for the bottle. Ramsay ignored her and took another swig. "Ramsay, slow down."

Maeve sighed. "We have to kill your sire. That's the only way to stop this."

Ramsay and Callie exchanged looks. Callie knew her brother. She knew him well enough to know he didn't want anyone dead, not even someone he barely knew, even if they were causing him pain and literally killing him. His heart was soft. Hers was, too.

But if killing Jabari would save Ramsay's life, she was willing to give it a shot.

"Here's the thing," Maeve said. "Once you die, you can still go back to being a human. It hurts like hell, but it can happen. The key is not to let your bloodlust take control and ruin everything for you. Once you've turned, you just can't drink human blood. But... to do that, yeah, you'd have to kill your sire." She let out another deep sigh. "So... for example, I don't want to be a vampire anymore, so I—"

"You don't?" Callie asked.

"No, honey. It sucks." Maeve continued as though she hadn't been interrupted, "Since I don't want to be a vampire anymore, and I haven't consumed human blood—as far as I know, anyway—all I'd have to do is kill my sire. Who... well, in this case, is our group's head vamp."

Callie nodded, brow creasing with worry. Elijah. He was the one who had fucked her up, too. Despite his charm and his gift of compelling, she was determined not to let him get to her again. She didn't want to become a vampire. She also didn't want to die. What she wanted to do was find a way out of this shitty situation. If that meant killing someone, so be it.

You do what it takes to survive, Callie thought. She was good at surviving.

"Once you turn," Maeve told Ramsay, "you'll want to drain every human you see. It's a hard urge to ignore. You'll want hot, live blood, and humans seem to be the ideal prey. But you can't give in to that, Ramsay. You don't want to starve to death, but you can feed on animals. Human food won't sustain you. You'll have to drink blood. Do you understand?"

"Becca would hate this," Ramsay said. "'Meat is murder' and all that."

"Becca would want you to be safe," Callie said. "Besides, you're not vegan. You consume blood all the time."

Ramsay shook his head. "Meat, Cal. Not blood. No one eats blood."

"Not 'no one,'" Maeve countered.

"Present company excluded." Ramsay took another swig from the wine bottle before passing it over to Callie. "I mean, if it'll stop me from starving or whatever, I don't have much choice. Hell, I'm glad Mom's not here because I could probably hear her pulse or some weird shit like that, right?"

Callie thought about hooking up with Maeve, how sensitive she'd been to Maeve's body, despite its lack of a pulse. How her hunger had driven her to think about blood. How *ravenous* she'd been for Maeve's blood, even while still drinking it.

Ramsay was right—their turning was inevitable. But slaking their bloodlust with human victims didn't have to be. They could stop it. If they worked hard enough, they could even become human again.

Human again, Callie mused. She was already becoming a monster, an inhuman killing machine. The idea made her skin crawl.

When she looked at Maeve, it was hard to see a monster. But all it took was one look at Ramsay's transformation to confirm that something bad was happening. They had to act fast.

"When it comes down to it," Maeve said, "we have to kill the sires. That will not only save you and Ramsay—it'll liberate T and me, too."

"And it'll save the town," said Callie. "The best vampire is a dead one. Present company excluded."

Maeve smirked. "So, we're doing this?"

Callie chugged the wine. It burned as it slid down her throat and coated her empty stomach. Ramsay was right, it tasted like shit. Still, the alcohol warmed her.

"We're doing this," said Callie.

Downstairs, the front door opened.

15

Callie and Ramsay started. Callie knew her mom had gone out with Derek, but she hadn't expected her to come back so soon.

"Expecting anyone?" Maeve asked.

"No men," Ramsay said. "Mom must've brought her date home."

"Derek," Callie said.

Maeve's eyebrow lifted. "Derek?"

"The guy from the boardwalk," Ramsay explained. Maeve's eyes widened. She stood and straightened her clothes.

"I need you to listen to me carefully," Maeve said. "I know Derek. He's not very nice."

"You know him?" Callie asked.

Before Maeve could elaborate, Susan and Derek turned the corner into the kitchen. Susan's hair was curled, and her pink lipstick matched her dress. Callie hadn't seen her cleaned up in a while. More than anything, she looked happy. That was what hurt Callie's heart.

She wished she'd never stormed out, that she'd been

much more supportive. Maybe she could've even helped her mom get ready for the date.

Susan's eyebrows lifted as she took in the three of them. "Callie, Ramsay... who's this? I didn't think anyone would be here."

Derek's gaze moved from Susan to Maeve, and suddenly lying to her mother was the last thing on Callie's mind.

"Maeve," Derek said. "What are you doing here?"

Maeve's eyes narrowed. "I could ask you the same thing."

Callie frowned. Okay, so they *did* know each other.

"I don't answer to you," Derek replied. His smile had twisted into a sneer. "You shouldn't be here."

"Callie," Susan asked, "won't you introduce me?"

"What's going on?" Callie asked Maeve.

"He's... the boss," said Maeve. "Elijah's father. He... well, he sired me. He sired all of us."

Callie balked. It couldn't be. "But the club," she said. "Elijah's blood."

"My blood," said Derek. "My son, after all."

Derek was a vampire. Not only that, but he was *the* vampire. The big bad she'd been searching for. It had never been Elijah.

Fuck, that meant her mother had gone out with a vampire. She'd invited him into their house.

"Shit," Callie hissed.

"What's everyone talking about?" Susan asked.

Callie's head and heart pounded. Derek had moved on to the kitchen counter.

"Lose something?" Maeve asked.

"Will someone answer me already?" Susan demanded. She stood next to Derek, but even he ignored her. Callie was terrified for her mother, but she couldn't say a word.

"I thought it would be nice to open the wine I brought,"

said Derek. "But it looks like the three of you have beaten me to it."

"Ramsay," Susan pleaded.

He couldn't answer, either. Callie noticed he looked more green than gray now, and his gaze was listless. His trembling had gotten worse.

"Only drank a little," he said. "Callie had..."

His voice trailed off then. His eyes rolled back in his head, and he crumpled to the floor. Callie rushed to his side, pulling his torso onto her lap. She smacked his cheeks, but he didn't come to.

"Ramsay!" Susan shrieked. She tried to push past Derek to get to her son, but he grabbed her arm and yanked her backward. She cried out in pain.

Callie's stomach churned. Blackness crept over the edges of her vision, and a profound sense of vertigo came over her. Shit. The wine. *It had tasted bloody.*

"Talk soon," said Derek.

Callie's muscles gave out, she slumped to the side, and everything went black.

16

Callie woke up not in her bed. Not in her house. She lay on her back in a pit. The darkness above and the humid air around her meant they were outside. Somehow, someone had put her there. Elijah stood at the edge of the pit leering down at her.

"Darling," he said. "So happy you could join us."

Callie was about to curse him out when nausea rose in her gut again, too pressing to ignore. She turned her head and vomited. Ashy bile coated the dirt. No traces of wine—that, or Derek's blood and whatever else he'd put in it. Callie wiped her mouth with the back of her hand. If he'd poisoned the wine, that meant he'd planned for her mother to drink it. Nobody fucked with her mother.

"How did I..." Spotting Ramsay's still form across the pit cut her off. "Holy shit. Ramsay."

Callie scrambled over to him, crawling on her hands and knees. Small pebbles and detritus scratched her legs and palms. His body was still, and his skin was pallid. He looked... well, dead.

She wanted to cradle him like an infant, but she didn't

even have the strength to lift him onto her lap. Whatever Derek had put in the wine had really done a number on her.

She brushed her fingers over Ramsay's face. He jerked awake and gripped her arm so hard, it felt like he wanted to break it. She gasped.

"You're hurting me," said Callie. He didn't let go. "Ramsay. Please, come on. It's Callie."

His pupils were blown wide—maybe with the drug? Callie wasn't sure. His irises were bloodshot to where they were more red than white, and his breathing was so shallow, it was like he wasn't breathing at all. That's when she realized he wasn't.

"Ramsay," she tried again. "Are you okay?"

But no, of course he wasn't. Neither was she. Maybe she looked as terrible as he did—they'd had the same wine. Somehow, though, she doubted it. Elijah still had said nothing else. He seemed content to peer into the pit and watch the two of them struggle.

Since Ramsay wasn't answering, she confronted Elijah instead. "What the fuck is going on here?"

They were so far down in the pit he had to raise his voice. "I thought you'd be curious. I just thought you might arrive at some conclusions on your own."

"What the fuck does that mean?" asked Callie.

"Your brother's one of us now—mostly, anyway. There's nothing you can do," Elijah answered. "Once he kills you, he'll be full-fledged. Dad had wanted you to join us, too, but the timing didn't work out. Don't worry though. We'll take good care of your family."

"Where the fuck is my mom?"

"Don't worry about her. She's with my dad now, and I promise you, he'll make sure she's happy forever."

Jesus fucking Christ. If she climbed out of this pit, she'd tear Elijah and Derek to pieces.

Callie's mind whirred to come to terms with everything he'd said. She and Ramsay had... what? Been drugged and dropped in a hole outside somewhere? Meanwhile, Derek had kidnapped Susan, too. What the fuck was he planning for them? And... why had Elijah said Ramsay would kill her? And why had he sounded so certain about it?

"He's my brother," Callie said. "He won't kill me." The tremor in her voice surprised her. Ramsay still hadn't let go of her arm. Maybe he didn't want to. She didn't want to meet his eyes and risk seeing a monster there, either.

What if Elijah was right? What if Ramsay *did* kill her?

Callie put her hand over her brother's and tried to pry his fingers off her, one by one. He growled low in his throat. The noise was inhuman. As she tried to pull away again, he bared his teeth at her. They looked sharp as fuck, like the fangs of all the other vampires.

She almost didn't recognize him.

"Ramsay, talk to me," she pleaded. "It's Callie. It's your sister."

"My sister is dead," he hissed.

Shock dropped like a bomb. Callie almost slapped him.

"I'll be back later to collect the leftovers," said Elijah. "Save some for the rest of us."

Callie didn't care that he was leaving. She was alone with a monster. He wasn't her brother anymore.

"I'm so hungry," he said. "So hungry. Your blood smells so good."

"Ramsay," she said again. "Ramsay, you can fight this. Don't give in just yet."

"I'm so hungry," he said again. "I can hear your heart racing. I scare you."

Cold sweat beaded on Callie's face. She couldn't deny it —he terrified her. If he had already turned, she stood no chance against him in a physical fight. If he wanted to attack her, she couldn't resist. All she could do was appeal to whatever part of him was still there and hope she got through. Otherwise, she and her mother were screwed.

"When we were kids, I was afraid of everything," she said. "You and Becca made me try so many new things. Think about that. Think about how it felt."

"Can't think," he said. "Can hardly talk. Really want to kill you."

Callie swallowed hard. The bloodlust would be a bitch for him to overcome.

"You don't want to kill me, Ram. I know you don't. You need to fight it."

He jerked her toward him, and she cried out, twisting in his grasp. Her arm popped out of its socket, shooting pain through her shoulder. Callie screamed. Even then, he didn't stop. He didn't let go of her. He'd dislocated her arm and if he got his way, he was going to bite her and kill her.

Hot tears streamed down her face. Her arm was numb, but the ache it gave off was excruciating.

"Ramsay, I'm hurt. I need to go to the hospital."

"Won't help," he mumbled. "It'll all be over soon."

With all her strength, Callie brought her other arm into his ribcage. He howled and released her, shoving her backward. Callie landed hard on her ass. She automatically threw out her arm to catch herself, and her body weight brought forth a fresh, searing hell that spread all the way to her stomach.

She vomited again, but there was nothing for her to throw up. Everything hurt like hell.

She didn't want to die. Oh God, she didn't want to die.

Callie cried so hard her chest hurt and she couldn't catch her breath. Her shoulder howled in agony. Ramsay pulled himself together and lunged forward to grab her again.

She rolled out of his reach right before he could touch her.

Ramsay growled again, rage burning in the gaze he fixed on Callie. Shit, she really didn't want to lose her brother too. Not like this. If she didn't do something, he was going to kill her.

"I love you," Callie said between sobs. "I love you so fucking much. Please don't do this. Please, Ramsay."

He hesitated, frozen in place. If he wanted to grab her, he could. "I might not have a choice."

Callie thought she heard a note of desperation in his voice. He really didn't want to kill her. His bloodlust was driving him to do the impossible, and he was still fighting it.

Callie looked to the top of the pit. Too high for her to climb, but Ramsay could make it. He could climb out and get help for them, maybe kill Derek and end it all.

But then, there was Elijah. They'd still have to contend with him. And a newly turned Ramsay was too weak to take on Derek. He needed Callie's help, even if all she'd be able to provide was a distraction.

She scooted farther away from Ramsay and something sharp jabbed her thigh. Callie recoiled. A broken piece of wood, perhaps a kind of frame, peeked out of the ground at a dangerous angle. A stake.

Callie wrapped a hand around the wood and pulled, but it stuck in the dirt. She hesitated before grabbing it with both hands and pulling as hard as she could, yelling in pain as the muscles and tendons in her arm flexed around the dislocation. The pain transformed into white-hot torture that forced tears from her eyes and a scream from her throat. Still, she kept pulling. She had to get it free.

Ramsay saw what she was doing, and his eyebrows shot up. "You're going to stake me?"

"No, not you," Callie said. "Help me out here."

Even if Ramsay was more monster than man, something she'd said got through to him. He hurried to Callie's side, wrapped a hand around the wood, and pulled it loose from the dirt without straining. The wood had broken off of a much bigger piece, with a point sharp enough to draw blood. To turn a vampire to dust.

Ramsay held the stake. He and Callie exchanged a look. His eyes filled with tears.

Callie's did, too. Maybe she'd misjudged his change of heart. Maybe he would kill her after all.

He moved toward her. She flinched, screwing her eyes shut, one arm thrown up to shield her from his onslaught—only, the pain never came.

Callie opened her eyes. Tears streamed down Ramsay's face. He was holding the stake out to her.

"I'm sorry," he said. "Whatever you want to do, I... I've made my peace with it." A hiccupping sob interrupted him. "I love you. You're my sister. Nothing that happens will ever change that."

Callie tried to swallow past the lump in her throat. Cautiously, she crept forward and took the stake from Ramsay's hand. She wasn't sure what her next move would be. She wasn't sure if she needed to kill him. All she knew for sure was that her baby brother had spared her, even not knowing whether she wanted to stake him. Knowing full well she could. Still, he had spared her.

Ramsay held her gaze while he yelled, "Elijah! Hey, fucker! Come see what I've done!"

Realization dawned on Callie like a second chance. She tucked the stake under her back and lay down on the ground. Ramsay tore at his arm with his teeth until a line of blood appeared. Before she closed her eyes, she saw him spread the blood all over his face and chest. He touched some to her neck.

Footsteps hurried to the pit. She felt Elijah's gaze crawl over her.

"Shit," Elijah said. "I didn't think you'd really do it."

"Shut the fuck up and get down here," said Ramsay. "I've almost fully drained her. Sorry, I couldn't help myself."

Keep your eyes closed, Callie thought. Don't breathe weird. Don't twitch. She couldn't give the game away, not when they were this close.

"God damn," Elijah said.

Rocks and loose dirt fell into the pit as Elijah clambered down. At least, that's what Callie imagined had happened. That was what she hoped. She made her breathing as shallow as she could, willing her body to look as close to death as possible. Just another minute and she'd be okay.

"Pretty thing, even now." Elijah's voice was low and smooth and way too close to her. If he wanted to reach out and touch her, he could. If he did, she wasn't sure she wouldn't flinch. "It's almost a shame."

"Almost," Ramsay said.

"How's she taste?"

"Exquisite. Come on over here and try some."

Elijah's footsteps crept even closer to her. An icy hand settled on Callie's thigh. She jerked, her eyes flying open.

Elijah pulled his hand back. "What the hell is going on?"

Ramsay set Callie down and grabbed Elijah in one motion. He moved with an inhuman speed. Callie could only hope he had the strength to match it. Otherwise, they'd never get out of the pit.

Elijah wriggled in Ramsay's grasp. Ramsay pulled Elijah in and held him tight against his chest. Callie tightened her hold on the stake.

She could kill Elijah if she wanted to. Put an end to all the bullshit. But... it wouldn't be enough. She and Ramsay both knew it. They still had to find their mother and save her from Derek. They had to stop Derek from killing again.

"Derek!" Ramsay yelled. "I'm going to stake Elijah! I'll stake your son! Come out here!"

Callie tightened her hold on the stake. Her heart beat so loudly, she couldn't hear herself think. She imagined plunging the stake into Elijah's chest and watching him explode in a cloud of ashes. She thought about doing the same to Derek, focused on the relief it would give her. She could use that power now to overcome her fear.

You got this, Becca's voice in her mind reassured her. *Right to the heart. It's time for us to end this.*

Derek appeared at the edge of the pit, standing where Elijah had stood. Since Callie's eyes were open and she didn't have to play dead anymore, she witnessed Derek's face as it shifted from anger to terror. His eyes blazed down at Callie, and he lunged.

Derek hit her like a train. The force knocked Callie down, away from Elijah. The stake tumbled away. Callie cried out, but Derek climbed on top of her and pinned her to the earth.

He showed her his fangs. "You lose."

Ramsay went for the stake, but Elijah slammed him against the side of the pit. They fell to the ground in a heap. Elijah kicked Ramsay hard in the ribs.

"Stop it!" Callie shouted.

"You can't make demands," said Derek.

If he was going to kill her, she needed an answer. "What did you do with my mom?" Callie asked.

"I'll give you your mother," said Derek. "But I'm not so sure you'll want her. After all, she's turning." The blood drained out of Callie's face.

"You didn't," she said.

"I did," said Derek.

"Fucker," Ramsay said. He clutched his sides and coughed. "You fed her your blood?"

"Had to do it," Derek said. "I put some in her drink at dinner. It was in the wine, too, but you wasted it." He scratched the side of his face. "Still, maybe I should be nicer. If we're going to be a family—"

"Who is?" asked Callie.

"You and Ramsay," he continued. "Susan, me. Elijah. Together for eternity. Doesn't that sound nice?"

Elijah stared at Callie. At one time, the heat of his gaze might have burned her. But now, she was way past fed up with his shit. His father was just like him.

"I know your dad walked out on you." Derek's voice was softer now, almost pleading. "You need a father figure. Shouldn't that be me?"

In her mind's eye, Callie saw her father. Suitcase in hand, standing in the open door, silhouetted against the rising sun. "Don't wake your mother," he said in a whisper. The goodbye she'd never gotten and how good it could've been. She thought of how it might feel to have a father in her life again. To have Derek as a dad.

She didn't need a father. She had her mother, and Susan was more than enough.

If they didn't do something fast, Callie wouldn't even have a mother anymore.

Elijah muttered something under his breath. Ramsay grabbed his shirt and pulled him down on top of him. Derek twisted his head to watch the chaos unfolding, and Callie saw her chance.

If she could just get to the stake.

Derek raised off Callie to curse Ramsay. It was the opening she needed. Callie rolled away from Derek and grabbed the piece of wood. Ramsay and Elijah kept him distracted enough that he didn't see her coming toward him with it raised above her head. Elijah did, though, and he froze. Ramsay froze, too.

"Callie," Elijah pleaded, trying to compel her. Another crawling itch, a warmth in the pit of her stomach.

"We had fun, didn't we? I never made you do anything you didn't want to. And... and if not for me, you never would've met Maeve." He licked his lips. "I know how you feel about her. I know you like her. Let me go, and I'll... I'll give you my blessing."

"I don't need your fucking blessing," Callie replied. "I don't need anything from you."

"You need your mom," Elijah countered.

"Callie," Derek added. "Think about what I'm saying. You know I'm right."

There it was, the crawling itch at the back of her mind. Derek was compelling her. Now that she was more monster than woman, he couldn't get through. At least, she wasn't making it easy for him.

And he'd turned her mother. There would be no saving her, not without Callie getting blood on her hands. Not without turning these fuckers to ash.

A wicked smirk turned Callie's lips. "I'm afraid you've tipped your hand," she said to Derek. "I'd say I hate to do this, but it wouldn't be true."

She exchanged a look with Ramsay and watched as realized dawned on him, as light filled his eyes and flowed into his smile.

Finally, she thought.

Ramsay shoved Elijah toward Callie, thrusting him into the stake. She caught the horrified look in Elijah's eyes as the stake impaled his chest. Power flooded Callie and steadied her hand as she kept the stake inside him.

Elijah burst like a balloon. There was no blood, only ashes. Callie let the wind carry him away. She felt no guilt then, only relief.

Derek's face went scarlet, and he roared as he ran toward her. The last thing Callie saw before she passed out was Ramsay as he jumped in front of her.

Her shoulder popped back into its socket and Callie sat bolt upright screaming. Ramsay held her in his arms and tried to stop her thrashing.

"Hey," he said. "It's okay! I fixed your arm. You're safe here."

Callie's scream died in her throat. She looked around. Ramsay was right. She wasn't in the pit. She was back home in her bedroom, with Ramsay and her mother sitting with her on the bed. Maeve sat in the chair by the window.

Bright sunlight streamed into the room, unimpeded by the blinds. The light warmed Callie's skin and made her mother's eyes sparkle as she looked at Callie.

Callie stretched to hug her mom. "God, I thought we'd lost you."

"Never," Susan murmured, holding Callie against her chest. Tears pooled in Callie's eyes and streamed down her cheeks. Her heart was so full, it felt like it would burst.

Ramsay put his arms around them. His cheeks were wet, too. As the three of them hugged, Callie realized she didn't feel like she was dying.

She pulled back to look at Ramsay. "Wait, is Derek dead?"

"Staked him myself." He didn't smile, and Callie knew it hadn't been an easy feat. Still, he'd saved her life. He'd saved Susan's life, and Maeve's. Even Tahlia's and Jabari's. God knew how many others.

Maeve got up and came over to the bed. Callie took her hand and laced their fingers together.

"You're free," said Callie.

"I'm free," Maeve echoed. "Guess you lost your vampire girlfriend."

Callie grinned at her. "But not my human one." She pulled Maeve down onto the bed with the others. Maeve stroked Callie's hair.

"Your mom knew about us the whole time," she said.

"No way," said Callie. "She didn't recognize you."

"She's talking about vampires," said Ramsay. Callie gaped at him and raised an eyebrow at her mother. Susan only nodded.

"We all heard the rumors when I was growing up," she said. "I thought vampires didn't exist. My parents didn't let me leave the house after dark, but I just thought they were overprotective." Susan shook her head. "Until Madison Cowell. She was my friend. I just assumed I'd never see her again."

"You didn't," said Callie.

"It was late one evening," Susan continued. "Autumn. I'd just left your dad at the college. I went to cross the street and Madison was standing there, just staring. She told me everything."

Callie's brow furrowed. It made little sense. If her mom knew vampires existed, why hadn't she said anything? Why had she never warned them?

"It's why they moved," said Ramsay. "Why we didn't grow up here."

Now, it made sense. Callie thought back to visiting her grandparents, weekends cut short without warning. Whole vacations spent in her grandparents' house, never going out past sunset. Susan's furtive looks outside.

"But why come back?" asked Callie.

"I had to try again," said Susan. "We couldn't afford a place in the city. Property values are good here, thanks to all the disappearances. The only thing about Neap Bay is all the goddamn vampires."

After everything else she'd been through, Callie accepted her mother's reasoning. Maybe it made little sense. Maybe it didn't have to. In the wake of losing Becca, Susan had paved the way forward. She'd saved herself, and both her children.

She'd even put herself at risk of becoming a vampire. Still, it had been worth it.

"I thought they all left," Susan continued. "I didn't count on Derek."

"Didn't count on me, either," said Ramsay. "Staked that fucker good."

Callie wished she could've seen it. Becca would've been so proud of him.

Susan swept a strand of Callie's hair off her forehead. "Jabari's gone, too. Ramsay chased them off."

"I couldn't kill him," he said.

"And Tahlia's fine," said Maeve. "She stayed back at the trailer. Human again."

Ramsay gave Callie a watery smile. "You owe me for saving the day, you know. You have to do whatever I ask you to now."

"Small price to pay," said Callie.

Ramsay leaned forward and squeezed her tight, hugging her until she groaned. For the first time in a long time, maybe they would be all right.

After a while, Ramsay and Susan left Callie and Maeve alone. The sun set over the house, bathing everything in orange. Maeve looked outside and smiled.

"You're stuck with me," she said.

"Me too," said Callie.

She scooted back against the pillows, pulling Maeve against her. They kissed. Her arm still hurt like hell, but things were looking up for them.

When they finally broke apart, Maeve threaded her fingers through Callie's. "Derek did a number on your family. I guess we all did. I'm sorry."

"It's okay," said Callie. "You just missed all the good stuff."

"Sorry for showing up late," Maeve said. "You all had one hell of a party."

Callie let Maeve put her down on the bed and pressed her mouth to hers again. She didn't pull away until she ran out of breath, and part of her marveled that she still had any breath in her to lose.

"You're right on time," said Callie. "We're only getting started."

ABOUT THE AUTHOR

Briana Morgan (she/her) is a horror author and playwright. She's a proud member of the Horror Writers Association and loves all things spooky.

As of 2021, Briana is the author of several novels and plays, including *Mouth Full of Ashes*, *The Tricker-Treater and Other Stories*, *Unboxed*, and more. She's a proud member of the Horror Writers Association and a book review columnist for the Wicked Library. When not writing, she enjoys gaming, watching movies, and reading.

Briana lives in Atlanta with her partner and two cats.

ALSO BY BRIANA MORGAN

The Tricker-Treater and Other Stories

Unboxed: A Play

Livingston Girls

The Writer's Guide to Slaying Social

Reflections

Touch: A One-Act Play

Blood and Water

Printed in Great Britain
by Amazon